GOTHIC PURSUIT

John Malcolm

GOTHIC PURSUIT

A TIM SIMPSON MYSTERY

Charles Scribner's Sons
New York

Charles Scribner's Sons
Macmillan Publishing Company
866 Third Avenue, New York, NY 10022

The drawings on pages 16, 104, and 153 are by Robert Staermose.

Library of Congress Cataloging-in-Publication Data

Malcolm, John.
Gothic pursuit.

"A Tim Simpson mystery."
I. Title.
PR6063.A362G67   1987   823'.914   87-12999
ISBN 0-684-18833-3

First American edition, 1987

2 4 6 8 10 9 7 5 3 1

Printed in the United States of America

GOTHIC PURSUIT

PROLOGUE

The *Cospatrick* caught fire at night on November 17, 1874, somewhere south of the Cape of Good Hope. She was a three-masted London emigrant ship of the Shaw Savill Line, with more than four hundred voyagers bound for Auckland, New Zealand. In those creaking clippers of an extinct era, fire at sea was a terror always in the thoughts of passengers and crew. This one started in the bosun's locker.

The standard procedure when such a disaster happened in the forward part of the ship was to get her head before the wind to prevent the natural draught from spreading the flames. At first this went well. The pumps were started and the crew began to douse the fire with water. Then, somehow, by mistake, the *Cospatrick*'s head got into the wind, fanning the blaze. The bosun's locker was full of oakum, rope, paint and varnish. Roaring flames burst out in terrifying gusts from below decks and ran up the tarred shrouds. Billowing clouds of choking acrid smoke enveloped the whole ship in confusing, blinding thickness. It became obvious that she was doomed.

The emigrants panicked. A starboard quarter-boat was lowered but, in their terror, a mob overfilled it and it capsized, spilling them into the ocean. The bow of the longboat caught fire as it was swung out over the rail, putting it out of action. Amid the shrieks and dreadful fear of 429 passengers and 44 crew, only the port and starboard lifeboats got away, with 42 and 39 people on board respectively. These lifeboats stayed near the unimaginable horror of the burning hulk for two days, until November 19, when the main and mizzen masts of the blackened, charred and smoking vessel fell on to the crowded after part of the ship.

Screams were heard from those crushed to the cindered decks. At the stern of the clipper the handsome Blackwall quarter-galleried glass panes were blown out by the dreadful pressure in a final explosion. The onlookers saw the captain, a luckless man called Elmslie, throw his wife overboard before jumping himself. The *Cospatrick* sank.

The survivors in the boats wore only their nightclothes and had no food or water, sails or equipment. One boat had only one oar. The other, with none, drifted away in roughening seas and was never seen again. Bad weather kept filling the boat that was left and, amid desperate baling, a sea-anchor was rigged. Men, women and children died in steady progression from thirst and exposure as the days passed. Those clinging desperately to life tore open the dead bodies around them, ate the livers and drank the blood. A foreign ship passed only 50 yards away in poor light and did not hear or ignored the feeble cries directed at it. Soon, there were only five men left: the second mate, called Henry Macdonald, two able seamen, an ordinary seaman and a passenger who had gone mad. This pathetic group were finally and miraculously picked up by another vessel, the *British Sceptre*, en route from Calcutta to Dundee, but the insane passenger and the ordinary seaman subsequently died, so there were, in the end, only three survivors.

We know what happened to the *Cospatrick* because Henry Macdonald gave evidence of the last of the old frigate-built ship at the inquiry. In other cases it is perhaps better that we remain ignorant for our peace of mind. The Shaw Savill Line was a bit unlucky with fires and disasters in its early days; it had fifteen sailings a year to New Zealand from London in the 1860s, with several fast little clippers that could still take four or five months to reach their destination. Many a tremulous emigrant, driven by courage or despair to seek a new life in the days before the Plimsoll Line, must have quaked as these little ships, mostly between four and five hundred, but none above one thousand tons, packed with people, beat round the Cape and then went eastwards into the Roaring Forties, where the passengers could clutch fearfully on to something fixed to steady themselves and listen to 'the whistle and scream of the westerlies on a dark and sobbing night'.

It was a hazardous business. The *Pleiades* and the *Halcione* were wrecked. The *Merope* burned off the River Plate on the homeward run. The *Caribou*'s cargo of coal caught fire in 1869, taking the wooden ship down in flames. The *Avalanche*, en route for Wellington with 60 passengers, collided with the *Forest of Windsor* in the Channel off Portland and only three crew members, who jumped on to the colliding ship, which also sank, were saved. The *Marlborough* just disappeared in 1889; no Henry Macdonald survived to tell the tale.

Eventually the passage became much safer and Shaw Savill, after merging with the Albion Line, became one of the well-established, highly-respected pillars of the British merchant fleet. Distinguished operations continued until comparatively recently, when the Furness Withy Group quietly absorbed the company. All in all, there was no particular reason why anything to do with the Shaw Savill Line should have disturbed the even tenor of anyone's ways until, quite suddenly this spring, an evil spirit from those fate-ridden 1870s came back to look for victims.

CHAPTER 1

She had the look of a woman who, the morning after, is not only confident of the role she has played the night before but feels that she has banked up an indefinable credit which can be called in at a carefully-timed moment. Her face, close to mine, was relaxed and beautiful in early morning repose, even if there were slight signs of that swollen languorousness one comes to recognize with experience. She gave me a meaning smile.

'I suppose you expect me to marry you, now,' she said.

I laughed. She's very fond of these role-reversal lines, culled from standing the conventional morality of a number of years ago upon its head. It made me chuckle but, in a way, I was both surprised and pleased. References to marriage are usually taboo with Sue; she has her reservations on that subject.

'Not at all,' I responded. 'Anyone who behaved herself quite so unreservedly as you did last night must be entirely unsuitable for matrimony. My mother warned me about girls like you.'

I won't say what she tried to do but I had to move quickly and I managed to grab her wrist in the nick of time. There was something of a struggle after that but it was interrupted, maddeningly, by the alarm clock bursting into a clamour far too late.

'Damn it,' I said, switching the ruddy thing off. 'I'd forgotten I was going to have a slight lie-in this morning. The place doesn't open until ten.'

'Serve you right,' she said, primly. 'I've still got to be at work on time, so you can get breakfast.'

I swung my legs over the side and put my socks on while

she disappeared into the bathroom. Normally I am well away before her because, despite what people think about merchant banks and the City of London, I do tend to get cracking before the Tate Gallery does. It's a bit further for me to get to the City from our flat in Onslow Gardens than it is for her to get to the Tate, where she's worked for some time now. I donned a large dressing-gown and set about getting breakfast with a degree of enthusiasm, for I was hungry and, although we don't go in for bacon and eggs with all the trimmings, we do rather like a bit more than a cup of tea—for me—and a beaker of coffee—for her.

In due course she arrived at the little table we have by a long window overlooking the gardens and sat down with an appreciative nod at the material I'd laid out. She was crisply dressed as usual, rather neat and buttoned-down, like one of those female executives with black briefcases you see in business hotels who cultivate the impersonal stare and the distant expression. Not that Sue ever carries a black brief-case: she has a sort of leather satchel-handbag into which she scoops everything, like a prep-school boy bundling homework and playthings together in an indiscriminate jumble.

'A boiled egg!' she crowed cheerfully. 'How nice! Where on earth did you find the eggcups?'

I gave her a reproachful expression. When you live with a girl like Sue there are great areas of domestic responsibility which are never defined, so that neither side can attribute blame for failure to perform. After nearly a year of happy cohabitation this situation had not changed but I was trying to exert some sort of control over her sway in the kitchen, where no sense of order seemed to prevail at all. I knew that it was almost useless, though I had my hopes, but I wasn't going to press the subject on one of the first warm mornings of April, when the sun actually shone into the gardens and spring might be going to happen if you didn't watch it too closely.

'The Victoria and Albert Museum,' she said thoughtfully, ignoring my expression. 'You and Jeremy are just like little boys really, aren't you? Any excuse for a trip out of school. Is there any real need for you to meet there? Let alone to drag Geoffrey Price in?'

I reacted with justifiable indignation.

'Of course there is! It's absolutely essential!'

'Why?'

'Why? Why? Well—er—we all have to be quite clear what it is we're talking about. Question of fundamental communications.'

Sue sank her white teeth into a crisp slice of toast. 'Nonsense. You could brief them at the office.'

I gaped at her, aghast. 'At the office? In the City? I most certainly could not! This is a matter for the Art Fund, Sue, not the Securities Department.'

She paused, holding a spoonful of marmalade above her plate. 'What difference does that make? You've got all your reference books, catalogues and photographs in your office there, haven't you?'

Her blue eyes watched me steadily as I picked up my teapot. Why do women always feel this need to challenge? If I'd been sharing the flat with an old College friend or an ex-rugger man he'd never dream of probing in this way. Never. He'd simply have said oh, off a bit late, are you, down to the V & A, well you lucky bugger it's the nine o'clock grindstone for me as usual, see you in the Dog and Duck for a pint around six, then? And I'd have said OK fine, I'll have one set up for you, and he'd have pushed off after taking an aspirin for his hangover. Simple as that. I gave her a scowl.

'It has become our practice—' was that perhaps a shade pompous, I wondered, but too late now—'it has become our practice to view and discuss in detail, indeed in depth, the next type of article we are going to acquire for the Art Investment Fund so that we are all quite clear and absolutely agreed on the decision taken. On these occasions—' I held up a warning teaspoon to restrain her, because she'd opened her mouth—'on these occasions I always make a sort of presentation to Jeremy and to Geoffrey, explaining the logic and the background to the investment so that they are both quite happy about it. One does not commit the odd hundred thousand nicker, or even just the possibility of it, lightly. Not in our business, anyway. I can't answer for the Tate Gallery, of course.'

That impressed her. She had been about to swallow some coffee and now she put her cup down. 'A hundred thousand? Tim, are you—are you serious?'

'Absolutely.' I didn't explain any more. It seemed to me that I'd done enough already. I filled my teacup and drank some tea with relish. She was still looking at me when I put the cup down. Christ, I thought, she's a good-look-ing girl, is Sue, but I should have known that glint in her eye.

'I thought you were going to be completely tied up with this timber thing that Jeremy has sicked you on to.'

I sighed. Trust a woman to spoil the morning. 'Now why did you have to bring that up? Eh? You know very well that I'm not pleased with this timber job, even if it does have historic significance for White's.'

I should perhaps explain that White's Bank was founded by an original merchant adventurer White in the early nineteenth century, importing rosewood from Brazil. Over the years White's had expanded into many other things and had become a proper merchant bank, if a bit idiosyncratic and specialized, but they had retained their timber interests. They still imported a range of hardwoods from their Brazil-ian company and, indeed, more recently, some softwoods too. They had a substantial operation in the Far East and Australasia doing the same thing, all handled into London. It was a good solid business, if a bit unexciting, and Jeremy had been taken aback when the other members of the Board had pressed him hard on a possible acquisition into distribution throughout Britain, requiring a commitment of capital into what Jeremy had always looked upon as part of the Bank's semi-colonial, possibly even moribund past. Jeremy White, you see, is something of a high-flier and a financial wheeler-dealer. He doesn't like industry much—in common with many of his City friends—and he'd rather gamble away on commodities and shares and securities and foreign exchange when he isn't setting up insurance schemes that avoid tax one way or another. So he'd tried to resist, but the Board for once had stuck to their guns and Jeremy, cornered, did what he often did on such occasions. He turned to me.

'You'd better look into it,' he'd said. 'You and Geoffrey, that is. It's right up your street.'

I protested vigorously. 'Damn it, Jeremy! We've just reorganized the whole Bank structure into proper departments! Geoffrey's in corporate finance and I'm supposed to be looking after overseas operations.'

'This is to do with overseas operations,' he responded gamely. 'The timber all comes from abroad, doesn't it?'

There's not much you can answer to that, so I'd been landed with the job as principal, Geoffrey offering moral and professional support. It hadn't pleased me; looking into a possible deal with a UK timber operation, possibly even having to buy it outright, needed careful research, assessment and risk analysis which, on top of other things I was doing, were unwelcome. I'd been sulky about it.

Sue gave me a wicked grin over the breakfast table but her eyes now showed concern. 'I think you're trying to avoid getting on with the timber thing, so you've lured Jeremy

out for a hooley.' She wagged a finger at me. 'I think it's a
diversion from serious business.'

I shook my head. 'Nonsense. The Art Fund may not be
more than an amusement for Jeremy and me in some ways
but it is a serious commitment of the Bank's to customers
wanting to invest in Art. When an opportunity comes up to
acquire something original, in the broad stream of our
policy, then we have to react to it. There's no playing hookey
on hoolies about it.'

She didn't say anything immediately but she finished her
coffee and she got up, tidied herself and got ready to depart,
satchel-handbag slung over her shoulder. She was wearing
one of the neat suits I always associated her with but
her blouse was open at the neck and she looked a real
heart-stopper, so important to me that I must have done
something odd or shown it in my face because she turned
back from her departure and came across to kiss me gently,
putting her hand on my flannelled shoulder to squeeze it.

'You and Jeremy have met at the V & A to look at
potential investments before,' she said. 'And you know the
sort of things that have happened.'

'Oh Sue! Now really—'

Her fingers, scented and warm, stopped my lips. 'Stick to
the timber business, Tim, please? Get the other over
quickly.' She took the hand away and walked to the door
before looking back. 'And come home early,' she said.

She didn't say why.

CHAPTER 2

Twin gables capped the edifice. Overlapping discs were
painted on the surfaces under the peaked tops, giving way
to stripes above the arched spaces under the gables, each

bisected by a turned column. An odd gallery connected the
gables across the rooftop, starting from the solid sides where,
at the front, bulbous turrets projected from the edge, rather
like those medieval turrets that bulge out from the four
corners of Scotland Yard, the old striped New Scotland
Yard that overlooks the Thames, not the new cement-
coloured New Scotland Yard off Victoria Street. Under the
gables were more massive, turned oak columns, fronting
shelves of heavily-bound copies of *Punch* and leather volumes
of indeterminate subject. Then there was a slope, yellow
with marquetry. Under that there was an incredible blocked
colonnade of Gothic arches, bound top and bottom by long
iron straps that were hinges; the whole colonnade was, in
fact, two great doors secured by a complicated iron lock.
Here and there, in a careful row, were inlaid discs of sym-
bolic patterns, like pies. Four small drawers, with iron
ring-pulls, ranked under the bottom iron strap-hinge. Then
there was a writing-surface, projecting out above more
columns with turned collars and a drawer. Beneath this
surface was a bottom cupboard, contained by two square-
panelled doors, criss-crossed with numerous stiles. The
whole effect was massive, mediæval, architectural, a cel-
ebration of jubilant ecclesiology and secular decoration. It
towered above us. I got Sue to do one of her architectural
sketches of it afterwards and even in that it came over as a
formidable creation.

'Good God,' said Jeremy White, his rich Park Lane tones
for once hushed with awe. 'It's more like a Town Hall than
a piece of furniture.'

Geoffrey Price gave a nervous giggle and looked quickly
round, like a schoolboy caught whispering in chapel. I
gave him a reassuring grin, as though to confide that the
respectably filtered light on the second floor back in the
Victoria and Albert Museum was not ecclesiastical and that
a distant, uniformed porter would not surge forward like a

churchwarden to hush his nervous rupture of the sepulchral silence. Around us stood the grave furniture of a distant age, most of it rather sombre. Only an occasional shine of bird's eye maple or satinwood, only the odd bounding scroll, spiralling into a query, broke the grained surfaces.

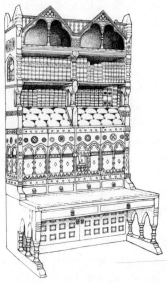

'It's supposed to be the most important piece of nineteenth-century furniture in the whole collection,' I said.

Jeremy shook his head in amazement. 'Furniture? Furniture? What on earth was it for?'

'It was his office bookcase. Cabinet. Call it what you will.'

'Office! Good grief! If I put that in my office at the Bank they'd send for the men in white coats.'

'It was an *architect*'s office,' I reproached him gently. 'And it was at the height of the Gothic Revival bit. Not that this is pure Gothic, of course. The circular motifs, pies and that, are of Japanese origin. He put his blue-and-white Oriental jars up in those spaces under the gables.'

'*Very* architectural.' Jeremy's sarcasm was heavy. '*Most*

necessary in an office.' His eye went up and down the aisle, taking in the various pieces, peering further inward to the gloom where William Morris's medieval cabinet, with its painting by Burne-Jones and others was ranged along the wall. I knew what he was thinking. Opposite the Morris, which had been exhibited with this very bookcase in 1861, were the Godwin pieces; the chairs, the tables and, more important, the sideboard. He gave me a scowl, telepathic as ever.

'Didn't have anything to do with Godwin, did he?' It was an aggressive question so I smiled back, blandly.

'Of course he did. They all knew about each other in those days. Not intimately; Norman Shaw wasn't a bohemian type at all. But there's Bedford Park; both worked on that.'

The scowl deepened. 'I'd hate to think that—'

'Of course not, Jeremy! This is quite different.'

Geoffrey Price cleared his throat, nervously. 'I think that what Jeremy is thinking, Tim, is that—'

'I know what Jeremy is thinking.' I didn't like to interrupt Geoffrey because he's a nice chap and an accountant, and you get your expenses paid by accountants, but this was between Jeremy and me. 'Jeremy is thinking that if I go off to locate this bureau-bookcase or cabinet or whatever it is, there may be trouble. Just because there have been one or two little incidents in the past.'

'Little incidents! Little incidents! Why—'

'The Art Investment Fund—' I raised my voice to overcome his indignation—'has made lots of purchases—correction, *I* have made lots of purchases for the Art Investment Fund—without the slightest hint of any problem whatsoever. There is no reason to suppose that this will be in any way different. None at all. If the cabinet exists, that is. If it is genuine. If—'

'All right! All right!' Jeremy was peremptory. 'There's no need to go on! Geoffrey is quite justified in his query. You

may recall, my dear Tim, that you and I agreed—once—
that no good ever seemed to come out of the Aesthetic
Movement.' He waved a hand towards the ebonized furniture, gleaming with silver hinges in the dusk nearby. 'Godwin and Wilde and Whistler, that whole Tite Street crew,
bankrupt and bumptious and—'

'Brilliant. I quite agree. What you have conveniently
forgotten, Jeremy, of our discussion in Brighton after that,
er, unpleasant imbroglio, is that we agreed that perhaps we
should have stuck to muscular, middle-class Christianity
instead of the atheistic Aesthetic Movement.'

His face wrinkled. 'I'm not having any of that Morrisian
nonsense in the Art Fund.'

'I'm not saying that we should. But we are not talking of
the Aesthetic Movement either. Richard Norman Shaw was
a sensible, professional, God-fearing Scot who became the
most brilliant domestic architect of the late nineteenth century. And this piece of furniture—' we all three swung
back to look up at its massive power—'is streets ahead of
Morris's.'

'It is incredible. Quite incredible. But do you seriously
think there is more of it about? Surely it would have come
to light by now?'

I shrugged. 'He got tired of this piece when he went off
Gothic. His daughter was in a convent so he gave it to them.
You wouldn't believe it—it turned up, completely forgotten,
in 1962.'

'Good grief. What must it be worth?'

'Ah. That's hard to say. My guess is into six figures. If it
ever came on the market, which it won't.'

'A hundred thousand pounds?' Geoffrey Price sounded
quite aghast. 'A hundred thousand? Jeremy, Tim is propos-
ing—'

'Not a lot, really.' Jeremy's murmur was quite ignorant
of Geoffrey's astonishment. 'Not for a major, unique work

like this. I mean, look at those Mackintosh pieces. Give me
this any day. Scotsmen might think differently, of course.'

'Shaw was a Scot. And the man who made this—to Shaw's
design—was called Forsyth. Another Scot, I suppose. But
any idea of price for this is pure speculation. My guess is
that although this is more important, much more money
would be paid for a highly-painted Gothic job by Burges or
one of those Morris pieces like that over there, painted by
Madox Ford or Burne-Jones, or both.'

'Burne-Jones! Burne-Jones!' Jeremy's voice was suddenly
full of contempt. He practically wheeled full round, sweeping
the gallery with a commanding, imperious glare. 'Man
painted as though he'd never seen a pair of buttocks in his
life.'

That's the amazing thing about Jeremy. Most of the time
he goes round behaving just like a typical City merchant
banking yahoo, as though Eton and Oxford had done
nothing but teach him how to sail, shoot and gamble. Most
of the time now he appears to be a classic member of the
Board of his family's Bank, White's Bank, addicted to
finance, insurance and horse-trading, loftily indifferent to
the world outside. Then suddenly you find he has a real eye
for a painting and has read extensively, read things you've
forgotten or locked away in your own memory-bank as
esoteric or indulgent.

'*Point Counterpoint*,' I murmured, hearing my voice isolated
in the hush of the museum.

Geoffrey Price stared at me, bewildered. Jeremy grinned
with pleasure at my spotting the reference: a statement
about Burne-Jones from the Bohemian artist-figure Bidlake,
based perhaps on Augustus John, from Aldous Huxley's
novel. It was just the sort of thing John might have said:
Burne-Jones's androgynous figures would not have been to
the liking of the old goat himself, whose perception of the
sexes was all too sharp. Jeremy clapped me on the back.

'Bravo! Let us have no truck with Morris and his circle. I hope Norman Shaw didn't?'

I shook my head. 'He knew them well, of course; he was in Street's office learning his trade at the same time as Philip Webb. And he used the William Morris firm, to begin with, for some furniture. But not for long. He said he couldn't afford to buy from a "socialist for well-to-do people". He exhibited this piece—' I gestured at the great bookcase— 'with Morris in 1861, but he was just getting started them. That was about it.'

'Good! Then tally-ho! After 'em, Tim! I like the idea of the Art Fund taking on a piece, a really important piece, by Norman Shaw.'

'If it exists.'

'If it exists, of course, if it exists. What a splendid find it will be!' He pulled himself upright majestically, allowing his tall blond figure to pose for a dramatic moment in the aisle as he waved a cautionary finger at me. 'If there's any hint of any trouble, though—any hint at all, the merest suspicion d'you follow me—you're to drop it, Tim. Do you hear?'

'I hear,' I said. 'I absolutely hear.'

Geoffrey Price pursed his lips as his eyes closed for a brief second. Then he pulled himself together and cleared his throat.

'I do hope there will be no complications,' he quavered. 'Really I do. But since you're both here and we are surrounded by the material, so to speak, do you think I could have a word with both of you—now—about the timber business?'

CHAPTER 3

The offices of that popular journal, *The Modern Façade*, are in Covent Garden. I reflected, as I strolled down William IV Street, cutting through from the Charing Cross Road, that this was very appropriate. The area north of the Strand has housed many publishers in its time, a lot of them involved with magazines of one sort or another. The area tends to attract advertising agents now, great phalanxes of the bullshit brigade, all dressed in trendy suits and quacking marketing platitudes as they scurry about with their folio cases full of artwork, but there are still some older, traditional outfits in residence. The Chatto & Windus building caught my eye on my way through to Chandos Place but that's a female preserve now, a case of the rib running Adam, so I suppose I didn't count it as I tracked on towards the office where, not too far from the operas he so dearly loved, Toby Prescott perched on the first floor above what had once been a vegetable wholesalers.

A girl stopped me at the reception desk, where back numbers of *The Modern Façade* were carelessly scattered with careful abandon, their brightly-coloured covers arranged in unconflicting chromatic order. As is so often the case with those involved with successful consumer goods and the media, there was a tinge of condescension in the way the girl received me, an impression that great patronage might somehow be conferred by your admission to the premises. I smiled at her unconcerned, since the boot was on the other foot.

'Toby's expecting me,' I said. 'Tim Simpson, of White's.'

He came barging through from his inner sanctum himself, mouth stretched in the familiarly broad frog-like grin I remembered so well, eyes bulging as ever, so that he looked as though he would be off, at any moment, to play the spoilt, aristocratic motorist in a local panto production of *Toad*.

'Tim! Dear boy! How are you? My goodness! You still look so—so muscular. Life at the Bank obviously suits you.'

I grinned at him in unashamed delight. You might not think that we had been contemporaries at College, but we had. Toby's few years more than mine entitled him to his avuncular style, not unlike Jeremy's; the reading of architecture at Cambridge is a much lengthier process than my modest degree had imposed, so that he seemed altogether to belong to a senior generation. In fact he wasn't quite forty. He wore a suit of a material that I would have thought of as definitely architectural in the modern sense: a grey, slightly knotty, slightly hopsack sort of cloth with a consciously woven texture to it cut in a style belonging to the cavalry, which clung tightly to his legs—my own itched at the thought of that rather tweedy contact—but had enormous fullness in the jacket flaps, as though to contain poacher's pockets. The effect was to enhance the Toad-image in a comically endearing way, to make a bulky grey ball of a body stand on narrow, strutting legs. A scarlet tie pouted from under his white collar, set on a red-striped shirt. His black brogues glistered with polish.

'You old *crapaud*,' I said, prodding him in the ribs. 'Who on earth d'you think you're fooling, hey?'

'Tim! Really! You can talk!' He shot a glance at the reception-girl, clearly entranced by our meeting, and I felt a pang of conscience at my lack of unction in front of one of his employees. 'You indeed! A merchant banker! I never knew such cheek!'

We both laughed loudly and he trotted me through a secretary's ante-room to his office, where two large windows overlooked the street. Despite what I've hinted there was a working atmosphere to the whole place, a profusion of coloured images, photographs, piles of copy, posters and bits of artwork stuck to hardboard. Along one side of his office, taking up a whole wall, was a huge set of bookshelves, full of very large architectural volumes; my eye caught works on Lutyens, Frank Lloyd Wright, the Adam brothers, Voysey, Hawksmoor, Casson, Corbusier and Siefert before I sat down, creaking, on a rather strange rush-seated Queen-Anne-repro corner armchair of racy style that Toby placed beneath me, beaming with bonhomie. He then trotted round to the other side of a large oak Gothic desk that separated us with pronounced serrated edge-moulding. I tapped it cautiously and cocked a querying eyebrow at him.

'Sedding,' he said, cheerfully. 'Almost certainly Sedding.'

'Not Seddon?'

'Aha!' He wagged a finger at me. 'Of course not! I'd have sold it to a museum and retired if it had been by Seddon. My goodness, Tim, you have changed!' His eyes, twinkling at me, were kindly as ever, but more respectful. 'It's true what they tell me, obviously.'

'What d'you mean? What's true?'

'Have some coffee?'

'Thanks. What's true?'

'Or would you—I say—what about a glass of, a glass of *white port*, now, with it?'

'Toby! We're not back at College, you know!'

He giggled. 'So what? Why are you so conventional, all of a sudden? You'd have said yes ten years ago.'

'Twelve,' I corrected him. 'I forgot that you were up for seven years, so these academic habits have persisted. Don't let me deter you, though.'

He pouted. 'You've spoilt it now. We'll just have coffee. It'll be better for us, I suppose.' He poured coffee from an elegant silver jug into bone china cups. 'You were such a *hearty* at College. All rugby and beer and pub-crawls. Now everyone says you're so knowledgeable about art and things. What happened? How did you do it?'

'Memory.' I took the bone china, refusing sugar. 'Just memory. I remember you told me once that memory and intelligence are not connected. Well, I got interested in antiques—my ex-wife did that—and then in art history so I read everything I could lay my hands on and memorized it. It passed a lot of time when I was travelling, staying in digs—I was a business consultant, remember—before I met Jeremy.'

'Ah yes, Jeremy. How is he? I only see him from time to time now. He's become such a tycoon. "Boom! the Banker of Bhong!" and all that.'

'He sent you his best. I hadn't realized you were well acquainted. What a small world.'

'Ah,' Toby's face went reminiscent. 'It's a while ago, Tim. After he left Eton. When he was at Oxford, actually.'

'Oxford? I didn't know you visited Oxford much.'

'Oh yes. My second year. Before you came up.'

Memory suddenly embarrassed me. I drank cautiously from my cup. 'Sorry, Toby, I remember now. The friend you had from—where was it—Sarawak? Wasn't he at Balliol or—'

His smile was kindly on my embarrassment. 'Indonesia. Java, to be precise. Taught me Dutch, Malayan and Tamil.'

'That's it. You introduced me once. Just after I'd come up. He was over from Oxford for the day. Christ, I was impressed. You were collecting languages like a schoolboy does postage stamps.'

His wide beam never faltered. 'I know. Which is why I cultivated you so assiduously, Tim, to start with. Your River Plate Spanish and your rather, er, individual Portuguese were so endearing. Of course—' he threw himself back in his chair and rolled his eyes at the ceiling—'once you'd become such a *famous* rugby player and got a *Blue* and become a sort of *God*, lesser mortals like me couldn't—'

'Toby! Pack it in!'

He giggled. The moment had passed; the painful memory had become a scar. It was hard, now, to remember his distress when the Indonesian friend had broken off with him, how he'd come round with me, cracking bad Spanish jokes as he drank himself senseless every night on appalling East Anglian beer until, in sheer compassion, I'd agreed to drink wine with him. The friends I'd played rugby with had looked at me a bit oddly at first, but once they'd realized it was just good friendship and superb conversation—Toby's experienced wit was on a level well above ours—quite apart from a crying need for company, they'd accepted him and liked him. Besides, no one was quite sure about Toby; sometimes he would bring the most magnificent girls up from London, Resting Actresses no less, and they obviously stayed with him at his digs and liked him and one or two were all over him, no mistake about that . . .

'You've gone all dark.' His voice startled me and I now saw his face again, the wide smile condensed, the eyes knowledgeable. 'You used to do that. You'd go off into a sort of trance and we couldn't get you back. Come on, Tim; have another coffee. I'm glad you haven't changed that much.'

'Thanks.' The mood had passed. I accepted more coffee and peered at his Gothic desk. 'Do you remember when you made me go with you to see the Handley-Read Collection? At the Royal Academy, years ago?'

'Indeed I do! Indeed I do! You hated it. The look on your face! It was a picture.'

'Well.' I smiled ruefully. 'I didn't know all about Burges and that lot then. Alfred Waterhouse—he was a pal of Shaw's, wasn't he? They all designed furniture. And they were all architects. Like Godwin.'

'Indeed they were.'

I looked at him. 'It was just before you started all this lot. Haven't seen you much since then. Tell me all about it.'

He shrugged modestly. 'Nothing much to tell.'

'Come off it, Toby! *The Modern Façade*! You're synonymous with success! Style, fashion, interiors—the whole Covent Garden bit. Nothing to tell!'

He laughed. 'It's true, Tim. Really. There's no money in it, you know. I looked round—mid-Seventies it was—and there were magazines on interior design, you know, women's things on *curtains* and that, and there were one or two very serious architectural journals and of course there was *Country Life*, but there was nothing in between. So I had the idea of starting a magazine, more town-based than country but not didactically so, which combined an architectural approach with something of interiors, something really exposing people to what style was all about and how architectural history fits in. I had a little lump sum, as they say. Started very small, very modestly, but I did have some lucky connections, people who were looking for something new, foresaw the Art Deco bit—'

'And you're a great communicator and you have the advantage of being extremely witty when interviewed, so the TV boys like you—and the girls—and you know half the architects who matter and most of the designers, so Bob's your uncle. *The Modern Façade*. Very clever and not at all easy.'

'Flattery will get you nowhere.' He was pleased. 'I work very hard and I meant what I said. I love it but there's no money in it.'

'Is that why we are being given a chance?'

'Of course. If I had the money I'd buy it myself.'

'Fair enough. Tell me about it.'

He smiled knowingly. 'First you tell me what you knew about him.'

'Richard Norman Shaw?' I waved a hand at the book-shelves and pointed at one book, a large paperback with a blue-and-white spine. 'I've read that. That's all. Oh, and Mark Girouard, of course.'

'Andrew Saint.' He got up and took the book out almost reverently. 'A great biography. Marvellously done. The Paul Mellon Foundation. Saint's biography of Shaw will stand for ever.'

'There's not all that much about furniture in it. I read it up yesterday.'

He gave me a sharp glance. 'There's enough. Certainly enough balance in the context of his career. Shaw was a great domestic architect, remember, not a furniture hack. You obviously didn't use your memory on this book so well.'

'Why not?'

He gesticulated at me. 'Open your knees.'

'I beg your pardon?'

He grinned. 'Don't get the wrong idea, you old Rugby thug. Open your knees. Look between them.'

The green corner chair creaked as I rather cautiously opened my knees, revealing the forward sharp sweep of the seat-rail and the swerving cabriole leg built into the front corner; the other legs were just turned and straight.

'What can you see?'

I gaped at him, perplexed. 'The edge of the chair. The seat rail.' I pressed back a bit. 'Rushing. My flies. What else should I see?'

'Look, Tim, look!'

I peered again. 'There's a stamped mark on the front edge. Chair must have been in an institution or something. It's—'

'Can't you read it?'

'No, I can't.' I peered closer, testily. I hate exams. 'It's just a stamped mark, a maker's mark or something. It says, let me see—Christ! It says R.N.S.!'

'Richard Norman Shaw!' we both shouted, together.

His delight was infectious. 'What else?' I realized that he had a marker in the book and was waving a photograph of the chair, clear on the page, at me.

'There's a sort of—sort of sunburst impressed above the initials. Just a few lines, like a Japanese flag.'

He nodded sagely. 'Sunbursts and pies. Sunflowers and scrolls. Symbols of the Aesthetic Movement. Sweetness and light. Victorian Queen Anne. A whole philosophy, Tim, a whole philosophy, lost and gone.'

I put my hand on the chair, reverently. 'You old bugger, Toby. Where the hell did you get this?'

'I bought it for a few quid at an auction in Kent.' His pleasure was smug this time as he handed me the book with the photograph. 'They hadn't the faintest idea what it was. Thought it was nineteen-thirties repro. In fact it's from Willesley. A farmhouse near Cranbrook that Shaw extended for the Royal Academy painter, Horsley.' He giggled. 'They used to call him "Clothes" Horsley because he disapproved of nudes. It was Shaw's very first country-house commission and it made his career.'

'And no one knew? About this chair, I mean? At the auction?'

'Nope. No one. Shaw was fond of corner chairs. They're very masculine. I keep that one here for enjoyment. No one has recognized it, yet.'

'Not me neither. I suppose I've failed the test?'

He laughed. 'You're in good company, Tim. A lot of so-called experts haven't given it a second glance.'

I stared at the photograph of the odd, curving chair, made to a design based on a Queen Anne, or at least an early eighteenth-century type, but somehow different. 'What sort of date is it?'

'Willesley? Eighteen-sixty-four.'

'Christ! I'd have thought this chair was much later. You

mean that they started Queen Anne repro as far back as that?'

'Shaw did. Interesting, isn't it?'

'Bloody hell. Makes you realize how little you know.'

'Drink deep,' he murmured, 'drink deep.'

'"Or taste not the Pierian spring."'

'Exactly.'

'Pope. I quite agree. Shallow draughts may well intoxicate the brain. May I now be guided? I've finished my coffee and am all agog.'

'Of course, Tim, of course.' He picked up an umbrella. 'Shall we go?' His eyes were twinkling and he was obviously enjoying himself. I had to clarify one last point.

'It's quite agreed, then? We will pay you a suitable, er, emolument as the finder and introducer of this piece if it does turn out to be genuine and we buy it?'

He nodded briskly. 'It's agreed. As we discussed on the phone the day before yesterday and as gentlemen. I take your word for it.' He opened the door. 'I know you, Tim.'

Not recently you don't, I thought, but still: a responsibility like that is tighter than five monkey-lawyers' contracts.

'Where are we going?'

'Not far, as it happens. Hay Yard. Just off Long Acre.'

'Heaven's sake! Is the piece there? So close?'

'No, I don't think so. Alf will advise us, provided all is in order and we give him certain, er, guarantees. As I explained to you, Alf is a failed architect but a fine bookseller, a technical man, who deals in architectural books and does a bit of design work on the side. He didn't get beyond his intermediate exams. He isn't actually in Long Acre itself— that would be too expensive—but he's in a passage off it. Quite a snug little place with a high skylight. Books right up to the heavens. He came into my office a day or two ago and said he was handling a piece by Richard Norman Shaw that was available. A cabinet or a bureau-bookcase; he was very defensive about details. Alf is always like that—gruff and brusque until you can open him up. Anyway it's like my desk, apparently; he gestured at it with a sort of stiff, casual wave that was so off-hand and mysterious that you wouldn't believe it. "That sort of style," he said. "It'll be a big price, very big. Architect's pieces always are."'

'He was right. Especially those nineteenth-century ones. Eastlake and Burgess and Godwin and Talbert. Not to mention Mackintosh, although he's twentieth-century really. But like your desk? You mean it's Gothic? Like the thing in the V & A?' I looked dubiously at his desk, with its rather attenuated Gothic influence, weakened by its distance in time from the 1861 Exhibition. The further away you get from Pugin the less impressed you are; Sedding was an architect whose offices were next door to Morris and Company and I guessed that the piece was made in the eighteen-eighties, when Gimson was articled there, well after the powerful Gothic Revival of the Sedding cabinet we had looked at that morning in the V & A and about which Jeremy had been so peremptory. 'Are you sure you can vouch for this, er, Alf? Does he know his stuff?'

'Oh yes! Indeed he does. A lot of people—dealers and the like—consult him as well as buying his books. I think that he was just indicating the style, not necessarily the detail.' Toby's voice came down to a soothing note. 'He's very knowledgeable but a bit, well, resentful, if you know what I mean. Thinks he was cheated in his Finals. I'm not sure that he wasn't; I know quite a few qualified men who haven't got half his expertise. It makes him brusque. I've given him quite a few commissions for the magazine and I've bought God knows how many books from him' He gestured at the shelves. 'Most of those, anyway. I don't think he'd come up with a cock-and-bull story. Not to me. You can't tell Alf anything about architectural history, not where this country's concerned. He has a world-wide mailing list.'

'I can't wait. Lead on, Toby.'

We strode out of the office and down to the street, Toby expounding on the architectural degradation of the area now that it was turned over to tourism. He moved surprisingly quickly considering his appearance and I was amused to stride alongside his briskly strutting legs as we eventually entered Long Acre about half way up, from the south side. No sooner had we done so than Toby turned right, south again, down a wide side-passage between two large shops. A well-painted sign pointed the way to Brown's Books and a door set in the left-hand wall where the passage opened out into yet a wider court repeated the same title. Toby knocked sharply and went in with me following deferentially, anxious to convey a good impresion to the man with the passport to a Norman Shaw piece. I had a sudden twinge of disbelief, as though no really important work of furniture could be forthcoming through so incidental a set of circum-stances, but then suppressed it; past experience had taught me lessons about the way valuable works of art get winkled out.

The first impression was of good daylight, surprisingly so for an inner court. Then my eyes went up vertically to the skylight Toby had mentioned, set high above me in a sloping roof about twenty feet up. The room was quite large, perhaps eighteen feet or so square, making the proportion pleasant. Books lined the walls and went on up to a gallery ten feet up, where more books could be seen lining the walls like an elegant library. There, however, the half-floor also contained a small drawing-office, below the skylight, with a draughts-man's drawing-board set up beside a folio chest.

On the ground floor, beside me, was a large table and, towards the back, a big office pedestal desk strewn with papers. However much Alf Brown might have resented his failure in his Final examinations, there was much about the whole set-up to envy; it was the workroom and bookshop of a neat, competent sort of man, a skilled technician of self-sufficient character, with an evident degree of professional discipline. I liked it. The only problem was that there was no Alf Brown in it.

'Does he know we're coming?' I inquired, perhaps not very tactfully, but I was keyed up. I always get tense before events like this, before big purchases or the possibility of them; it's part of the excitement, the sort of fear that suffuses the system with nervous anticipation.

'Of course he does.' Toby looked around and then up at the drawing-board work-platform above us. 'I told him yesterday. Alf?'

He wasn't irritable or snappy or anything, just slightly perplexed, and he wandered, without showing too much concern, over to the big desk with its papers strewn about. He clucked his tongue. 'That's not like Alf,' he said, 'leaving papers muddled like that. He's always so neat. He—'

I had been looking curiously at the rows of books, big volumes many of them, pretty valuable in some cases, that lined the wall near me up to the place where the stairs rose to the cat-walk above. It was the way Toby suddenly stopped that made me look up to see him, head turned to his left, frozen at the big desk with his slightly bulging eyes opened wider than usual. I couldn't see what he was looking at because it was under the stairs so I walked across to him, to his left side and looked, following the direction of his gaze to a point under the stairs that had been concealed from me.

There was a man lying down there, staring at us. He was slightly built and his legs were stuck outwards, twisted in a way that must have been uncomfortable. His face didn't move.

'Alf?' Toby's voice was full of surprise at first, incredulity, as though he'd found a maiden aunt in bed with the milkman. 'Alf? What are you doing? Are you all right?'

Alf didn't answer. I didn't expect him to. It's very difficult to answer when your head is over at that angle because to get that way your neck has to be broken, broken severely enough to ensure that you are dead. I know, you see; I've seen that angle a couple of times before.

'Alf?' Toby's voice had lost its incredulity. It was hoarse now, and full of fear.

I knelt down beside the late bookseller to check that he was dead. He was, and he hadn't fallen from the gallery above because to get where he lay he must have been propelled very violently across the room. What little learning Alf Brown had possessed about architecture had turned out to be a very dangerous thing indeed.

CHAPTER 4

Sue did a turn up and down the flat. She actually wrung her hands. It's a condition you often read about but never seem to see in real life; a person wringing their hands together in agitation, elbows stuck out, knuckles whitening, the odd joint cracking. Her eyes glared at me. Her breathing was rather short-winded.

'I did get home early, as you asked,' I pointed out. 'Look on the bright side, if you can. I've made tea for you.'

Her mouth opened and closed. No sound came out.

'There didn't seem much point in going on to the Bank,' I went on, gloomily. 'Jeremy would only have been upset.'

'My God! Jeremy! Is that—is that—all you can—'

'It took a long time, I must say.'

'What? What took a long time?'

'Oh, you know, for people to arrive and all that sort of thing. You remember Motcomb Street? A bit like that. Then we all had to go off to a police station—Holborn, it was—

and there was all this taking of statements and interminable explaining to do. It's no wonder they have to keep on recruiting more policemen. The bureaucracy is unbelievable. I can't understand how any of them actually get out on to the street. Well, they don't much, do they? They have everything set up for putting into computers now, you know, it's like being at an airport, telly screens everywhere and people typing at keyboards. That's where they dug up Nobby, I suppose.'

Sue stopped her pacing, bang centre in the middle of the carpet. 'Nobby? Nobby Roberts? You mean poor Nobby has had to be dragged into one of your scrapes? Again?'

I looked up at her indignantly. 'What do you mean, *poor* Nobby? There's nothing poor about Nobby, let me tell you. Chief Inspector, inflation-proof pension, lots of praise from Maggie Thatcher, plenty of tea to drink, minions cringing about kowtowing like blazes, and then usually someone else like me has to do it all for him.'

'Oh no! Oh no! No you're not!'

'Of course I'm not.' I tried to be soothing. 'Just a figure of speech. I mean I just had to, before. Not now. I can't really say that I'm delighted to be sort of *known to the police*, if you get me, but that's evidently what happens when they punch my details into the box. A flag goes up saying refer to Chief Inspector Roberts, Scotland Yard, and that's what they did. And before you could say Bob's your Uncle round came Nobby in a white Rover, old Plod in person, irritable as a singed porcupine, he was.' I chuckled. 'Didn't half take him aback to see Toby.'

'Toby.' A new look had come into her face, a sort of meaning look, if you know what I mean. 'I might have known that—tell me—Toby's never married, has he?'

Strange how women bring up these irrelevancies.

'No.' I kept it casual. 'No. He never has. Why?'

'Nothing.' Her voice carried a thousand shades of meaning. 'I just wondered. He's obviously a friend of yours, so you'd know.'

'Oh, I'm sure I must have told you before. Never has. Not the type.'

'The *type*?'

'You know Toby, very intellectual, cultivated, a bit donnish really, loves the opera, food, wine, mad on his magazine, married to it, not a family type at all. Detests children. No, not the marrying type.'

She pursed her lips. 'Well. I'm not the one to discuss old friends of yours.'

'Really? I thought we'd discussed old Nobby many times.'

'That's different.'

'Different? Because he's a rugger player too or because he's happily married to Gillian and loves his kids and all that—that—'

'What?'

'Domestic you-know-what. Have some tea?'

She scowled at me. I could tell that we were getting off the subject and into deep water. Sue's conviction that I constantly get into the sort of situation we had had in Long Acre really won't stand statistical analysis but it is unfortunate, I must say, that one or two odd occasions like it have happened before. She was involved in the first one, in Motcomb Street, and in another in Chelsea, which she took rather well. She's fond of Nobby and Gillian, very much so, despite the fact that Nobby can be extraordinarily prickly about himself and his job, a sort of moral vocation it is, no sense of humour about it at all. You wouldn't think we'd been at College together sometimes. He was a cracking good wing threequarter was Nobby, twelve years back, and went on playing for a lot longer than I did.

'I take it that Nobby and the other policemen involved warned you—very seriously—to let them handle everything, absolutely everything, connected with this man Brown's murder?'

'Oh yes. Absolutely. If it is murder. To the point of tediousness. Repetitively. Toby became quite restive about it. I don't think he and Nobby would get on very well now, you know.'

'Did they ever?'

'Oh—well—they weren't exactly *close* but they were quite congenial at one time. When I was with them, anyway. Years ago.'

She sat down and picked up the cup of tea I'd poured for her. She drank a bit, put the cup down, bit her lip and tapped her foot on the carpet. Then she stared at me before she spoke. It was the sort of stare I don't like; it had the look of a schoolmistress about to address a mob of recalcitrant schoolchildren to whom she feels an ultimatum is due. I hate being treated that way: I'm very bad at learning lessons.

'Tim?'

'Yes.'

'I'm going to have to say something to you.'

There was a pause. I could have screamed. I'm not a child to be put through responses. I waited.

'Are you listening to me?'

Her voice betrayed tension. '*Mirame quando le hablo,*' I said.

Now she glared. 'What does that mean?'

'It means, "Look at me when I'm speaking to you." Latin schoolmarms are just the same as ours.'

'Tim! I'm serious! If you don't leave everything—*everything*—to the police and keep out of this dreadful business I will leave you. Do you hear? I will *never* come back. Is that clear? I've a mind to pack now.'

'I hear you,' I said. 'Don't pack. Please don't pack.'

'I mean it! You attract trouble!' Sue held up an imperious palm to check me because my mouth had opened. 'I know what you'll say! It's not your fault, you'll say, it just happens. Well, this time it's going no further. Nowhere.'

I spread my hands. 'How can it go further? I know nothing of Alf Brown. Never met him. Not involved. Feel no emotion about him.'

'The bookcase! I know you. You'll want the bookcase. It'll be a challenge to you. Please, Tim, *please*, I beg you, yes, I beg you, let the whole thing drop.'

I sighed. I bet the first person to think of saying the pledge was a woman. Public commitment and apology: they're mad on them.

'I don't see that I have any choice. The trail began and ended with Brown. Toby can't throw any more light on things so what else can I do? I have no forensic skills and I'm not interested in avenging Brown's death. It might have been quite unintentional; manslaughter, not murder. I have a pile on my plate with this timber business. There's no time.'

She wasn't convinced. I could see that she wasn't convinced, but there was no point in going on because she'd never believe me, would she, and I'm damned if I'm the sort of man to make public declarations, professions of faith and intent; I won't. She picked up her cup and saucer again and gave a long-drawn-out moan.

'If only I didn't know you so well,' she said, with rather more dejection than I liked.

CHAPTER 5

'Tell me,' I said to Nobby Roberts, putting a pint of bitter down on the pub table in front of him, 'why have you been lying to me for the last two or three years?'

His lean, sandy face checked as he peered at me. A stiff

look set into his gingery, freckled features and his muscular jaw closed tight for a moment before he spoke indignantly. 'Lying? Me? To you? Bloody cheek! When I think of how you've behaved and the trouble you've got into! How I've had to compromise myself over and over again while you've avoided telling the truth! What do you mean? Eh?'

He's quite ungrateful, is Nobby. To hear him talk you wouldn't believe what I've done to help him solve cases that have added to his swift promotion. Like all moralists, Nobby suffers from the delusion that it is his character, the strength of his purifying convictions, that have led to his elevation, quite apart from the sheer hard work and unremitting motivation that have moved him since we left college together. Because we were such close friends in those days we've never really drifted apart since, but Nobby looks on me rather like an early Christian with his beady eye on a sinner: if only he could dissuade me from my way of life he thinks that I might Join the Throng, if you follow me. To him, my defection from business consultancy, which had a degree of evangelical activity associated with it, and my move to stewardship with Jeremy and White's Bank constituted a Fall from Grace. Merchant banking, to Nobby, is a mercenary, unprincipled, low-down form of usurious swindling that is more appropriate to a lounge lizard than to a decent, hardworking, productive, stalwart, taxpaying citizen of the realm.

He's probably not far wrong.

'I mean,' I said, sitting beside him and taking a first cooling swig from the jug, 'that you've always given me the impression that you were in the Fraud Squad and you're not.'

'Eh?'

'Don't act innocent! You had to come over from Scotland Yard yesterday. I found out that the Fraud Squad—the real Fraud Squad, that is—are in High Holborn. You have never

been stationed in High Holborn. Ergo, you are not in the
Fraud Squad. You have deliberately misled me. And others.
What are you in? Special Branch? Or daren't I ask for fear
of salt mines?'

He looked quite defensive. Attack is the only way to deal
with Nobby, otherwise he swamps you in moral fervour. He
bridled a bit before he spoke. 'I did not say I was *in* the
Fraud Squad. I may have conveyed that impression, but—'

'Oh yes you did! The Art Fraud Squad. I remember it,
definitely.'

'I said I was *attached* to the Fraud Squad. On special
duties. You are quite right; the Fraud Squad proper, the
one that deals with financial and, er, City-related matters,
is in High Holborn. I am not, structurally, a part of it.'

'Structurally? What amazing minds you coppers have.
How is your structure today? Not too rigid, I hope, after
your unpleasant surprise yesterday? Frightfully formal you
were. I mean, I understand that you have to maintain your
proper position, your rank and station, in front of all those
mere constables but you were very stiff with Toby. I'm used
to it, of course. I understand that you don't really mean it
when you're so bloody rude, but he was quite put out. Old
College friend, senior police officer, turns up loyally when
old pals are being sniffed at by woodentop bloodhounds and
instead of clapping all and sundry on the back, beaming
bonhomie, the old "Don't worry, Sergeant, these gentlemen
are friends of mine, can vouch for them, pot of tea and some
fairy cakes on a tray'll do fine," you go all sniffy and cold
and—oh splendid, she's brought our Ploughman's.'

There was a pause while the barmaid set down two plates
in front of us, each loaded with the regulation doorstop of
crusty bread, slab of Cheddar, scoop of butter and about
half a pound of pickle and chutney, without any of those
wisps of lettuce and watery slices of tomato that some pubs
seem to have become infested with. For once Nobby looked

quite approving: his face softened with interest and his mouth, which had become grimmer, curved outwards in the beginning of a smile.

'A proper Ploughman's,' he murmured. 'I must remember this place.'

We were in a pub south of Trafalgar Square that I had chosen, partly out of previous experience and partly because it was not too far for Nobby to walk but out of range of his colleagues in Broadway. There was silence for a moment or two while we both tucked into a preliminary mouthful and then he managed to speak, working the words round a hefty compendium of bread, butter, cheese and pickle.

'I don't know how you do it,' he mumbled. 'Actually, I've given up getting upset about it. You're a sort of magnet for corpses. Especially if they're involved in the fine art trade.'

'Well, you should be happy. It's your specialization, isn't it?'

He shook his head. 'It *was* my specialization. It's not now, not more than a watching brief and my past experience being available.'

'Oh I see. Well, I'm sorry if I've dragged you back to your murky past. What are you supposed to be doing now?'

He scowled. 'I do not have to reveal what duties I am undertaking now.'

'Ho! So that's the tone. Proper procedures and complete discretion, is it? Investigating one of our cabinet minister's relationship with a Bulgarian masseuse, are you?'

'I certainly am not!' He grinned suddenly. 'I wish I were. Might be more interesting than what I'm doing. Contrary to popular belief, a large amount of police work is very dull.'

'There you are. I try to make life interesting for you and all I get is dog's abuse.'

His eyes looked at me steadily as he munched further into the bread and cheese. 'Talking of relationships, I'd no idea that you'd kept up with Toby.'

'I hadn't.' I bit off a chunk myself. 'I hadn't seen him for years. Heard of his progress, of course. *The Modern Façade*, very *à la mode*. But then he contacted us a few days ago. About this piece by Richard Norman Shaw that the late Alf Brown had put up, like a gun-dog. You know the rest; it's all in the statements. It was great to see Toby again: he hasn't changed. None of us have..One never does.'

'Hm. You always liked Toby, didn't you?'

'Of course. Brilliant chap. Architecture, languages, culture. Learned a lot from Toby.' I picked up my beer-glass.

'We often wondered. You were such good chums for a while, at College.'

'We often—' I put my glass down. 'Now what do you mean by that?'

'Don't get excited! I'm not inferring anything, you know, untoward. Just that it was an odd mixture, you and he, that's all. Nothing else.'

'Now see here, Nobby—'

'No! No violence! You must know what I mean. We all knew you were absolutely straight, my God, it was obvious, but Toby, well, we were never quite sure what was what, were we?'

'You were pleased enough to know him, your first year. Short memory you've got. I can recall one Saturday night down Mill Lane when one of the lush girls he'd brought from London took a shine for you and you nipped outside with her and—'

'Tim! No!' Breadcrumbs sprayed the table.

'—found you in the meadow, skirt up round her ears and you going at it like a—'

'Tim! For Christ's sake! People will hear! Stop it!' His agitation was comic. 'That's the past! The past! Can't you ever forget anything?'

'No. To be honest. Biographical detail is something that sticks in my mind. All I'm saying is that we had some

hilarious times together in our first year. After that, of course
things changed. We were into rugger and we didn't see that
much of him any more. Of course I know what you mean.
Maybe Toby was—is—ambidextrous. It's not my business.
I've always liked him for what he was to me; witty, generous,
sophisticated. He's a mine of information and he's very well
connected.'

'With more than one social world.'

I gave him a sharp glance. 'Ah. You've obviously started
your inquiries. Very quick off the mark.'

He stroked his glass thoughtfully. 'That sort of outfit,
Tim, a semi-fashion, semi-serious magazine; think of it.
Connections in printing, advertising, design, journalism,
architecture, art, bookshops, paper, distribution, photogra-
phy. A concentration not only on buildings but on objects,
things, materials, even landscape gardening. Almost anything, in fact, connected with a household. Brings in all
sorts, doesn't it, and needs a man as—versatile?—as Toby
Prescott to keep it all together. Quite a selection of talents, in
fact. Used in several different worlds and rubbing shoulders
with all sorts. Did Toby have money?'

The question was abrupt, short, taking me by surprise.
'No—I—no, I don't think so. He said he started *The Modern
Façade* with a small nest-egg, but it doesn't make any money.'

Nobby's mouth gave a twist. 'That's all relative, Tim, as
well you know, being a banker. We'll know what he means
from the accounts, anyway.'

'Why? Why are you digging into Toby? He didn't do it,
that's obvious.'

He raised his eyebrows. 'Is it? You said yourself it didn't
take long to get from his office to Long Acre. The full report
won't be available for a while but Brown had been dead for
a few hours. Whoever it was visited him around opening
time and no one else seems to have been into the shop until
you arrived.'

So there it was, I thought dully. While Jeremy and Geoffrey and I were standing in the Victoria and Albert Museum gazing at the Gothic bookcase, talking about it, someone did in poor Alf Brown almost as though our voices, our decision, had sent out vibes that set off the deadly process.

'Not much sign of an argument,' Nobby mused. 'Papers on the desk ruffled and searched. My guess is that Brown knew his assailant. Perhaps a customer. Not afraid of him, anyway. He was struck a few blows and then got the one that did it. People don't realize how fragile we are sometimes. All that cinema-cowboy trash. If you hit a man the way John Wayne was supposed to in some of his films, especially if the recipient wasn't expecting it, you'd very likely kill him or maim him for life. Brain damage, anyway. Brown wasn't strongly built. Broke his neck on impact with the wall. Unlucky for the attacker, perhaps.'

I know, I thought, I know, and you know I know. Well, not all of it you don't and I'm never telling you: mine was in self-defence.

'Have another beer?'

'Just a half, thanks, Nobby.'

'Same here.' He shuffled off and I finished my plateful. A mental image of Toby rose to reproach me. He had kept his nerve remarkably well, but then Toby was no panicker. I'd left him in the bookshop while I summoned a policeman. Toby had been sitting alone, shaken and pale, when I came back but he was composed. We talked to each other briefly while more officials arrived. At Holborn they had taken our statements separately but we'd waited about together quite a bit. We were both comically apologetic to each other, feeling an individual responsibility for what had happened. The ebullient mood of our meeting earlier had seemed blasphemous; in a way I felt as I imagined a drunk driver does after a hilarious party which has ended in a smash and his presence in the cooler. What a mess, I thought, what a mess; if we had been about to renew an old friendship its rebirth had been most nastily blighted. Once Nobby had arrived it seemed worse; there had been Nobby's disapproval and uncertainty, his official position, his exasperation to contend with. He had been pretty cool with Toby. Nobby's very square nowadays, very moral; it must be something they do to them at Hendon, but I was willing to forgive him that because his heart is in the right place and you can depend on him. In a way he was now keeping very calm and friendly compared to the outbursts I've had from him before; perhaps, I thought, he's reached a philosophical accommodation with my tendency to get involved in these things.

He arrived back with the half-pints and gave me a rueful smile. 'I bet Sue gave you an earful when you got home?'

'She did. More in sorrow than in anger, though. "Nanny is not cross, she is just very, very disappointed" sort of approach. Much more effective in many ways.'

He laughed. 'You are a dreadful man, Tim. All I hope is that you'll be sensible this time and keep out of it.'

'Of course.'

He gave me a sharp glance. 'You've said that before.'

I spread my hands. 'Could I help it? Could I?'

'Yes.'

It was my turn to laugh and give him a silent toast as I lifted my glass to sip the first sip. 'Touché and cheers.'

'Cheers. And that goes for Sue, too.'

'What does?'

'Keeping out of it. You dragged her in last time.'

'Now that's unfair and you know it. She insisted.'

'Only because she wanted to keep tabs on you, what with your reputation and all. I'm telling you, Tim—'

'I'll come to a bad end? You've said that before, too, but here I still am.'

He sniffed as he put his glass down. 'Well, I wouldn't call White's unsurious Bank a good end but we'll not squabble on that subject again. You've made your bed, Jeremy White's bed as it happens, so you can lie on it. Just don't expect me to scrape up any gory remains, that's all.'

'God, you are becoming a dour old bugger, Nobby. There isn't any Scots Calvinist blood in you by any chance, is there? Or Wesleyan? You'd have made a good companion for Carlyle or Knox, you would. You could have sat moaning together about the misery of man's ways and really cheering each other up with a glass of fresh water. What are they doing to you at Scotland Yard?'

A grin came back to his face. 'Depressing me, it's true. I'm sorry if you think I was a bit strong with Toby Prescott. Actually, Tim, it was almost a relief to get called out to Holborn and know that you were misbehaving again.'

'Me? Damn it, Nobby, I'm not—'

He held up a hand. 'All right! All right! Don't get violent! What I was going to say was that I'm bogged down with paperwork and technical stuff, which stultifies any keen policeman because although someone has to do it the real job is out there. Out here.' He glanced round the pub. 'So I'll keep a distant eye on the Holborn crowd, won't offend them, and I'll let you know what happens.' He held up a finger. 'Please, Tim, please, I *beg* of you; keep your distance.'

'I will. I promise. I'm off to the Tyne for two or three days so you can't keep much further distance than that, can you?'

He stared at me gloomily. 'Alaska would have been better,' he said, 'but I suppose the Tyne will have to do for the moment.'

CHAPTER 6

I'm not going to bore you with the timber business. Britain was once covered in the stuff, just a vast forest, but what with random domestic heating, cooking, houses, wooden ships and charcoal for smelting iron there hasn't been much left for the last two or three hundred years so we import most of it. A lot of the softwood comes from Scandinavia and gets in through the east coast ports. From further afield softwood and hardwood come to places like Liverpool and Cardiff, but London still handles huge quantities of both, so it's not as though White's were out of the centre of things. When the other directors demanded action of Jeremy and he passed the ball on to me, Geoffrey Price went into a great gloom and started quavering on about the best use of our money and whether we shouldn't conserve management resources. I had to tell him, somewhat briefly, that I wasn't charmed with the subject myself but that a job was a job and I might as well do it thoroughly. He mumbled disgruntledly as he dug out a folder on Edwards & Coe, timber merchants and importers, giving it to me with a shake of his head.

'If only Jeremy had kept his mouth shut this would never have happened,' he grumbled. 'Bloody yachtsmen.'

I cocked an eye at him. 'Yachtsmen? What have they done? Sunk Jeremy's boat?'

He gesticulated at the folder. 'You'll see it in there. You know that Jeremy keeps a boat on the Hamble. Well, so does Sir John Coe. Head of Edwards & Coe. Lives in a big pile in West Sussex when he's not here in the City. Convenient for their operations at Shoreham; Shoreham's a big softwood port now. He and Jeremy met on the Hamble.

Next thing you know, Sir John Coe's putting up the idea of a merger of our timber interests, or even a takeover or something. Jeremy blabs about it in the Bank dining-room, never thinking anyone'd take it seriously, and here you are or rather here we are, pair of us, up to our ears in bloody woodwork. So the great wheels of industry grind on.'

'Ever smaller.'

'Ever smaller. To dust or, in this case, to sawdust.'

I shook my head at him. 'Mustn't be negative, Geoffrey, and especially not with humour. Places like the North-East are swimming in timber. From what I hear, Coe's crowd are very strong up there and not too dusty elsewhere outside London. We are pretty much concentrated here. He may have a point. Put us together and who knows?'

'Who knows indeed? We're not the only ones who can put two profitable operations together and lose a fortune. Just try us.'

There's no dealing with Geoffrey when he's in one of those moods so I left him, clutching my folder, and got to work. Edwards & Coe seemed to have extensive interests, depots everywhere, a transport company and no Edwards. Of the originators, only the Coes remained. I gave a cursory glance at the list of directors, sighed at the balance sheets, and decided to start as far away as possible and work my way back. I got hold of Sir John Coe's secretary, fixed appointments of a very discreet nature, told Sue I'd be away for a couple of nights, got out the Jaguar XJS and tooled off up the Great North Road determined to get it all done in the quickest and most efficient manner possible.

I got to Immingham first, took a look at the Humber, scouted the Edwards & Coe operation and then went back a bit to Scunthorpe. After that, Goole. I said I wouldn't bore you with the timber business and I won't. The next stop was Hartlepool. I spent a night in Newcastle, looked at South Shields and then, for no really pressing reason, went to Blyth, which is where the temptation happened. Up to then I had been behaving logically and dutifully. I worked hard, taking copious notes, and listened to those I interviewed respectfully. My head was stuffed with timber, its handling and its markets. It was at Blyth, after I'd looked at the docks, around lunch-time, that I realized I'd seen all I was going to and, instead of keeping my head down to the grindstone, I raised it, quite in disobedience to Sue, who I'd 'phoned the night before and assured of my good behaviour. She said she was going to bed early after tidying up the flat, which was so much more controllable in my absence and I said yes, men are trouble, and she agreed. I left the conversation at that and heard her laugh to herself as she put the phone down. Well, at least she's cheered up a bit, I thought, probably because I'm out of danger for a few days or at least out of mischief and she can make arrangements to fix me properly when I get back.

It all goes to show that there's just no telling. I sat in the car at Blyth, where it had turned damned cold by midday, with the freezing rain that April gives to the North-East bursting itself and its sleet on my windscreen and suddenly, from musing about tonnages and cubic metres, containers and veneers, my mind ran on to what the stuff is used for: furniture. From furniture it wasn't a far hop to bookcases and Norman Shaw, with something I'd read somewhere in Andrew Saint or Mark Girouard rustling the wet flat leaves rotting themselves to fibre under the dark trees of my brain. A tingle of apprehension went through me. I've never really wanted to seek for trouble, you must understand that, but there are things, unfinished things, necessary connections, nagging queries, that will not let the mind rest, over which I have no control. I hate unanswered questions. I was in Blyth, you see, where the road signs indicated the way back down to nearby Tynemouth via Seaton Delaval and to

Newcastle; that was one way. The other way was to Bedlington, Morpeth, and further north.

Morpeth, that was what did it. I looked at my watch. Not yet one o'clock. I had a mental image as I closed my eyes of old black-and-white photographs of panelled rooms with arched or panelled ceilings, heavy, containing furniture that was either gravid sideboard oak or spindly, thin-railed chairs, ebonized in dusty black like all Aesthetic Movement furniture based on the Japanese. There were two or three of these old black-and-white image-photographs: in them I could see a rich patterned carpet on the floor and expensive wood going up the walls or, in one case, plasterwork arching to the great window-ceiling of a picture gallery. Below, on the heavy carpet, was furniture; in one case furniture lined the walls just like the paintings.

'Cragside,' I murmured out loud, to the noise of icy rain drumming on the roof. 'Of course.'

The car seemed to know the way. Once round Morpeth you take the road further north towards Rothbury, where the National Trust now direct you carefully round the 1,700 acres that Sir William Armstrong planted with millions of trees, until you are wound in among them as you enter the country park. I drove carefully through the huge conifers that block the light until, at the end of the tarmac, beyond the intervening trunks, I could see the astounding house, piled teetering above the Alpine-style gorge of the Debdon Burn in a landscape that seemed to belong more to the Black Forest than to Northumberland.

I use the word house, but the hunting lodge that Richard Norman Shaw converted to a country residence for the inventor and armaments manufacturer Sir William Armstrong is more like several houses to look at, welded together into a huge and solid and well-kept mass, with an extraordinary medley of impassive stone walls, calm Gothic arches, half-timbering of black-and-white brightness and sharp red roof-tiles, capped by a tower with a strange, timbered hutch-roofed top to it, stuck like a miniature Swiss chalet above the rambling concourse of buildings that make up the total called Cragside. I sat in the Jaguar, pulled up in the gravelly earth of the car park carved from the sloping hillside and the trees, gaping at the sight around me until, by force of habit, I got·out to stretch my legs and ease a bad knee I inherited from a collapsed scrum in a long-distant rugger match. Still stooping to put the key into the door-lock, I glanced up over the car roof and caught sight of a big Ford Granada estate with a trade rack on it, about six cars away in the line. There was a movement which had caught my attention as the driver opened his door to get in. His back was turned to me but I could see he was a tallish, slender man bulked up by a blue plastic anorak. His check trousers went down to a pair of unmistakable brown suedes with rubber soles. I nipped round the back of the cars and, as he got in, I clapped a hand on his shoulder.

'Gotcher!' I exclaimed, cheerfully.

He gave a great start, dropped his keys, cursed mildly, leant on the horn, jumped at the blast and twisted round to gape at me.

'Christ! Tim Simpson! You bugger—I nearly had heart failure.'

'Guilty conscience,' I replied, grinning. 'All you Brighton Boys are the same. Antiques and women: you're all guilty.'

He gave me a reproachful glance, put his leg out of the door and emerged, blinking, to stand up and shake hands with me. Stan Reilly is not really one of your typical Brighton Boys. By that I mean he is not a chunky, cockney-accented, aggressive bloke who waves fivers in your face. It's unfair to quite a lot of the Brighton trade but I'm afraid a section of them have produced that image: tough, unrelenting, confident coal-heavers with a reputation for rapacious door-knocking. Stan is one of the other sort; rather thin, almost weedy-looking, and tall, but quite stringy and resilient, with a hatchet-shaped narrow face like an inquiring bird or a curious librarian, almost ascetic but slightly skew. When he speaks his voice is quiet with a faint Sussex accent emphasized by the use of local phrases like 'made up', to mean pleased. 'I heard you were made up with that,' he'll say, meaning he'd heard you were pleased with it. The gentle manner is deceptive; his shop in Hove is a pleasure to visit because he always has something unusual or attractive in it and you have to be sharp to keep that up. Stan has always been a bachelor as far as I know, so my remarks about women were of no relevance to him; antiques were his obsession and he never seemed to need close relationships of any sort. He shook his head at me.

'You are a terror, Tim, really you are. What on earth are you doing here? England isn't safe from you any more.'

I chuckled. 'I didn't think this was one of your stamping grounds either, Stan.'

'Everywhere has to be a stamping ground for a poor, hard-working dealer like me these days. Everywhere. Goods are so hard to find. Don't tell me you're buying up the National Trust now?'

'No. Not me. It is a long way from London, I agree, but it's even further from Brighton. Sorry, I mean Hove.'

It should be explained that Brighton and Hove, in the manner of south coast towns, have run into each other until, to the stranger, they are inseparable, rather like Hastings and St Leonards. In the same way, Hove rather fancies itself as a bit superior to its more famous neighbour and resents being lumped in together with it in any casual geographical reference. Stan's shop is just into Hove but a chance visitor, moving west through the tangle of streets, would never know where the borderline lay. He gave me a cautious smile.

'It is,' he admitted. 'But I've done a run up to the North-East many times before, Tim. I'll say no more.'

Etiquette dictates that a dealer keeps his sources of supply to himself unless he volunteers them. It is bad form to press him on the subject of where he buys; not only bad form but commercial ignorance. Older dealers often used to help new ones by telling them of the good 'calls' in a certain area but with increasing competition this is becoming less common and, in any case, auctions are steadily replacing other dealers as a source of supply. I nodded sagely and changed the subject, gesturing at the pile above us.

'Culture time then, Stan? Come to see how the great men used to live?'

He nodded quietly, following my glance up to the gables. 'Quite something, isn't it, Tim? Quite something. You can't imagine anyone having the money to build a place like that now, although I suppose it still happens in America and the Middle East. I've just stopped off to do a tour, for interest, like. Might learn something, I thought. Have you been round it? Before, I mean.'

I shook my head. 'My first visit, too. I've been up on business—not antiques business, Bank business—so I just thought I'd take a gander on spec. Playing hookey really.'

He laughed, looking over me carefully and keeping his eyes on mine watchfully. 'Lucky man. You're not thinking of buying the place for White's Art Fund or something?'

'Oh no. Once in the National Trust, forever in the National Trust. We can't buy Cragside. What's it like? Inside, I mean?'

He wagged his head up and down with affirmative pumps of the neck. 'Quite something. Really quite something. Well worth seeing. I had no idea what it was like. Armstrong must have been a remarkable man. He must really have liked contemporary art, too. But see for yourself.' He waved a hand at the great house. 'I've had my lunch-break: much too long a lunch-break. Won't say that it was wasted, though. You always learn something when you visit these

places; you get a better feel for the furnishing and design of
the period. You get to understand a bit better what they felt
was the latest thing. It always helps.' He smiled gently. 'I
suppose they'll say the same about a David Hicks room in
a hundred years' time.'

'I suppose they will.'

He held out his hand. 'Nice seeing you, Tim. Take care,
now. I must be off. There's a good call I can make before
this afternoon's out.'

'All the best, Stan.'

He retrieved his keys from the car floor and I watched
the big Granada lumber over the bumps to the surfaced
road, where it straightened itself out and then slid off
towards the house, disappearing under a wide, pointed stone
arch in the side wall. I strolled after it thoughtfully; it was a
long time since I'd seen Stan and I knew of his bookish
interest in all old things but somehow it felt odd to meet
him there, in the cold damp forest on the rocky hillside by
the house. It seemed incongruous to mix the reality of
Brighton's commercial trade with this carefully-preserved
tourist attraction. A spatter of rain hit me and I shivered as
I hurried to the entrance.

The interior is quite staggering but I'm not going to make
life tedious with a guided-tour monologue on Cragside. The
room that sticks in my mind the most is the library, which
was finished in 1872. It is panelled in oak to a height of five
feet and has a beamed and coffered ceiling. Between the two
there is snuff-coloured wallpaper. On the wallpaper hang
Pre-Raphaelite paintings, which are another story in themselves, but I was looking for furniture, of course, and, despite
the distractions of Morris stained glass designed by Rossetti,
and gilt panels with painted leaves, and blue-and-white
porcelain, I saw plenty of furniture.

There was no Gothic bookcase, though.

There were ebonized black chairs with cane seats and

leather back-panels stamped with gilt and pomegranates. There were red leather sofas. There was a Gillows writing-table and there were even four corner chairs of 'Queen Anne' style but not quite like Toby's green one. These were pitch black in shiny ebonizing, more stolid, and they had stronger back legs with turned stretchers between for added strength. The front leg was a cabriole though, like Toby's green one. The back slabs were painted and the seats had leather coverings, not rush, gilded again, like the other chairs in the room, so that they were very decorative as well as being very masculine. It was a glorious room, the room of someone who really liked art, and it made me begin to understand what most of the Aesthetic Movement had tried to do and failed, whereas Shaw had succeeded magnificently.

I explored the rest of the rooms enthusiastically but there were no more clues to the existence of other Gothic bookcases or pieces like the one in the Victoria and Albert Museum. Nothing like it came into sight. This house and its fur-nishings were a different exercise, something else, a move-ment onward in style and taste. I collected all the information the bookshop had in print and got back into the car. Serve you right, a little voice said, for doing your terrier-act again; you've wasted your time. No, I haven't, another voice replied; time spent viewing places like this is never wasted. Tucked away in the memory-bank now are impressions that will never fade, just as Stan Reilly said, or something like it. The pleasure of that library was worth every minute of the trip. And the corner chairs, they were great, I thought, I must remember to tell Toby about those. When things have died down a bit, of course.

CHAPTER 7

If you put your foot down it takes five hours or so to drive from Newcastle to London. I let myself into the flat in Onslow Gardens some time around ten. Sue was sitting in front of the fireplace, on the big sofa, with her legs curled up under her, reading. She put her book down hurriedly and scampered across to greet me with considerable enthusiasm. After a while I let go of her and we went into the kitchen to brew a pot of coffee while I foraged about for something to eat. Sue tends to be a health-diet faddist, so when I had found a beefburger, three sausages, eggs and a clod of cold mashed potato she gave me a reproving look.

'I'm not cooking that for you,' she said. 'There's some salad things and the remains of a fish stew you could have.'

'That'll do to start with. While I cook the sausages.'

She shook her head sadly but before I had been tending the grill for long the fish-stew-salad appeared in a bowl with some dressing and I wolfed it down, chatting lightly to her about the attractions of Scunthorpe and the treeless rawness of Newcastle. She quizzed me quite closely for a while and it wasn't until I'd finished my miniature grill and we had taken our coffee into the living-room, where she regained the sofa and I had a sprawl in one of the armchairs, that I realized she hadn't said much about herself, apart from asking me to note how tidy the flat looked.

'What about you?' I demanded. 'Surely not two whole days and nothing to report?'

'Oh no,' she said, 'it's been very quiet. Two full days at work and two early nights in bed like a good girl.'

'Some chance. Alone?'

She pulled a face at me and I grinned, reflecting that

there had been no need to mention my visit to Cragside, although I would very much have liked to have discussed its contents with her. Sue is not very keen on Victorian romantic painting or, come to that, on anything very much of the decorative side of the British scene before 1890 or so. French Impressionists, now, that's another matter: Sue is an expert on them. The big picture gallery at Cragside, like the vast drawing-room with its enormous marble double-storey chimneypiece, originally had Armstrong's Victorian paintings in it, with work by Millais and the superior Pre-Raphaelites, all sold off in 1910. Cooke was present with his marine painting, and Horsley, through whom Shaw got the contract to design Cragside for its famous owner. I sipped my coffee. Shaw must have enjoyed himself hugely with that house, just as Armstrong did. The library I had liked so much was the first room in the world to have permanent incandescent electric lighting, powered by a hydro-electric generator that Armstrong had connected to a turbine, driven at the dam he had erected to form Debdon Lake. The whole thing was an enormous play-castle for a man with unlimited private funds; the work that was done on the grounds, rearranging huge rocks and planting vast forests, was a major occupation, quite apart from the interiors that Norman Shaw had so carefully considered for his client. Thinking of him and of Cragside, I quickly decided that I'd have another glance at Andrew Saint's book, and Mark Girouard, some time when Sue wasn't about, just to check my facts. It wasn't that the temptation to persevere had dominated me—not yet—but intellectual curiosity needed to be satisfied that I hadn't missed something in my tour. So, while smiling at Sue over my coffee-cup I shot a quick glance at the big set of bookshelves on the wall opposite where we jointly kept a great range of books on fine art and related subjects.

The Andrew Saint wasn't there.

Still smiling, I looked quickly back at Sue to make sure she hadn't noticed the direction of my gaze and answered a banal question of hers about Jeremy and Geoffrey's attitude to the Coe's timber operations. As she half-turned to put her coffee-cup on the side table parked by the settee I took a much longer, steadier look at the place on the bookshelf where Saint's biography of Richard Norman Shaw, with its distinctive blue spine lettered in white should have been. Then I let my eyes range right along the serried volumes before looking back, just in time, to intercept a glance from her.

It definitely wasn't there. Nowhere in the bookcase.

Finishing my coffee, I eased myself up to my feet and stretched luxuriously, as a man who has driven solidly for five hours and then eaten needs to do, flexing my bad knee before I put the cup and saucer down on the mantelpiece beside me. The April night was dark outside and it was pleasant to look at the room, with the paintings assembled separately by both of us hanging carefully on the free walls. Behind me, over the fireplace, was the big coastal marine by Clarkson Stanfield that Sue didn't like so much; in front, my Seago next to Sue's Stanley Spencer. To my left was a wall containing an etching of Dorelia by Augustus John and a Picasso print. Elsewhere my Wilson Steer had to contend with all Sue's ladies: Sylvia Gosse, Laura Knight, Elizabeth Stanhope Forbes, Dod Proctor and Ethel Walker. It was a nice room, calm, unperturbed and unruffled: I liked it. I smiled down at Sue, with her shoes kicked off and her feet tucked under her, propped against the arm at one corner-end of the sofa. She smiled back.

'You must be tired,' she said.

I eased myself off the mantelpiece, took a step across the hearthrug and sat in the middle of the sofa next to her knees and feet. 'Not that tired,' I said.

A look came into her face, the sort of look that said

ho-hum he's been away and now that he's back and he's
fed he thinks that the next logical step is a bit of you-know-
what but he's not just going to do that, oh no, I'm not
having that. Still smiling at her, I slid my hands along the
sofa, one on each side of her, so that I was leaning over her,
bringing my face close to hers.

'Tim! Now look here—'

Too late. Slumping down on her as though to impose a
kiss and pinning her body beneath my chest and shoulders,
I slid my hands right to the end of the sofa and then up and
under the cushion supporting her back. My right hand
hit something hard and I grabbed it, pulling it out and
straightening myself up with a triumphant shout as the
bright red-and-white photograph of Scotland Yard on the
cover of the large, chunky paperback came into view.

'Well, well, well,' I crowed. 'Fancy that! What have we
here?'

She straightened herself out, flustered, pulling her skirt
back over her knees and smoothing her woollen sweater
down.

'You bastard,' she said.

'How extraordinary. *Richard Norman Shaw*, by Andrew
Saint. Under the cushion at the back of you. Most odd.
Quite peculiar. I wonder how it got there. To bed early,
you said? With a good book, perhaps? What a funny thing
—especially after your little homily to me three days ago.'

She scowled blackly. Her mouth set in a line. Guilt
emanated from every bit of her expression. I wondered if I
might not have cause to regret this little victory but suppressed the idea: I was too pleased with myself just then.

She found her voice. 'All right, Clever Dick. I've been
reading it. So what?'

'Curiosity killed the cat, that's what. So what were you
looking for?'

She pouted. She's a very pretty girl and I love her, but I

managed to sit severely on the middle of the sofa, away from her feet.

'Get me some more coffee and I'll tell you,' she commanded.

I went through to the kitchen with our cups, replenished the coffee and came back into the living-room. She was sitting more upright and had tidied her dark-brown hair carefully. Her large blue eyes looked at me without blinking. She has a slenderish figure but with a good bosom and her lips are full. I handed her the cup of coffee and she sipped it before speaking so that I could admire her for a brief moment.

'I had to make a decision,' she said.

'Decision? What decision?'

She pointed at the door. 'Whether to walk out through that door, bag and baggage, traps packed, or whether to stay.'

'Walk out? What on earth are you talking about? Why?'

'You know very well why! Don't think I don't know you! I've either got to be a part of your hopeless love of snooping or pack up! It was the same with the Whistler business. Either I'm a part of your life, Tim, or I'm not. I'm not going to sit here like the meek little woman while you gad about chasing that Norman Shaw cabinet and get yourself killed. I'm not! So do you want me to stay?'

'My dear Sue, sweetheart, of course I—'

'Well then! I'm not that much into architectural history but I do know a bit about it. I decided to bone up on Norman Shaw. I was keeping it quiet for a bit. Until you asked for help.'

'Thank you for making that decision,' I murmured courteously, 'but I do feel that your getting involved is a bit—um—well, Nobby nearly killed me for endangering you over the Whistler. This is quite different, of course, but—'

'But nothing. Blow Nobby! I really think I must have a

word with Gillian. His attitude to women is so old-fashioned.'

'Perhaps she likes that.'

I got a withering glance. 'I had no doubt that you wouldn't leave the matter with Nobby and the police. So I'm going to be involved, Tim. That is, if you want me to stay?'

'Of course.'

'Good. What did you think of Morpeth?'

I gaped at her. 'Morpeth? I never said I'd been to Morpeth.'

'Of course not. But you did say you'd been to Blyth. So naturally you must have slipped up to Morpeth too; it's very near. On the way to Rothbury.'

'How did you know that?'

'Oh, Tim, really! I have an Oxford degree and a diploma from the Courtauld!'

'Not in geography. I didn't go to Morpeth. There's a bypass.'

'Now stop it!' A reminiscent look took over her face. 'If you really want to know, I once had a boyfriend up there.' The look went smug. 'A very good boyfriend too.'

'A Geordie? I didn't know you liked a bit of the rough in your younger days.'

'You are insufferable sometimes! He was not a Geordie. Not in the sense that you are inferring. His family had large estates in Northumberland.'

'Wild country. Full of strong silent men.'

'He asked me to marry him. I'd have had a large farm and my own hunter by now.'

'A horse? How very boring.'

'There is nothing wrong with horses!'

Horses bite at one end and kick at the other, but there's no telling Sue. A horse is the most bone-headedly violent animal you can think of, liable to take fright at a gesture intended for someone a quarter of a mile away and kick its

owner to death as a result. In England they ride horses on
hard thin saddles and hold the reins with both hands, which
is ridiculous. Where I learnt to ride in South America they
put a sheepskin on the horse first so that the saddle sits like
a club armchair and you only hold the reins with one hand,
as does everyone else in the world. It leaves the other hand
free to wave your sombrero or fire your revolver. I decided
to say nothing; Sue has that English girl's sentimentality
about horses which defies all logic.

'You'd have been bored stiff. No art to speak of.'

'There was plenty of art at Cragside.'

'Huh?'

'Cragside. You did go there, didn't you? It was inevitable.
Was there anything there that gave you a clue?'

I put my cup and saucer back on the mantelpiece, crossed
the rug again, and sat down beside her on the sofa. 'No,
there wasn't. And I'm glad I'm not married to you,' I
said.

'Why?'

'Because if I were your husband I would feel considerably
endangered by a wife with such prescience, or insight, or
whatever it is. I wouldn't feel safe.'

She smiled. 'It didn't take much calculation,' she said.
'Once you'd mentioned Blyth I was practically home and
dry.'

I leant across and kissed her gently. 'So we're quits?'

'Quits.'

'Sue, please don't do anything I don't know about, will
you? Please?'

'Don't worry. I'll let my big strong bodyguard know
everything. Providing he does the same.'

'Done. It's a deal.'

'Then I reckon it was for Nesfield.'

'Eh?'

'The cabinet, Tim.' She became brisk. 'That's what we're

after, isn't it? A Gothic cabinet or bookcase like the one at the V & A? Shaw designed that for himself in 1861. Well, what about Nesfield? They set up office together, Shaw and William Eden Nesfield, in 1863 or so. They were partners in architectural practice, two famous men together for about three years, later on. In 1869 they split up the partnership but continued to share offices. What could be more natural than that? Nesfield might have admired Shaw's bookcase and asked him to do another one, maybe the same, maybe different?'

I sat back from her. Once she gets the bit between her teeth, horses have nothing on Sue. 'There's only one thing wrong with that,' I objected.

'What?'

'Nesfield was as famous as Shaw, to start with. Perhaps even more so. He designed a lot of furniture, I seem to remember, which has all disappeared, but he was a well-known furniture designer. Surely he would have designed his own office bookcase?'

Her mouth turned down a bit. 'Oh dear. You've got a point, Tim. I just naturally thought, since they were so close in the eighteen-sixties, that the only other person Shaw would have produced a cabinet for would have been Nesfield. They were so influential together.'

'The Old English and Queen Anne styles, you mean? Possibly. But they worked quite separately. Nesfield was a bit of a *bon viveur* and mixed in different circles to Shaw. I have a feeling he died youngish.'

'Fifty-three.'

'Eh?'

'In the late eighties, eighteen-eighties. About eighty-eight I think. Cirrhosis of the liver. He was fifty-three.'

'How odd. What a coincidence. Godwin was fifty-three when he died. Also a *bon viveur*. Like Sir William Orpen. Also a *bon viveur*. Remind me to be careful in my fifty-third year. The ladies and the drink were prominent in all three cases.'

She gave me another of her looks, the sort that ignore what you've just said while registering it for future use. 'Anyway, I believe Nesfield's furniture was not unlike Shaw's. They even designed some together, I think.' She brightened. 'Suppose this is one of those pieces? Designed by Shaw and Nesfield together?'

'That would be a coup!'

'Wouldn't it? Oh Tim, how exciting!'

He face flushed. Her eyes sparkled. I couldn't help feeling her enthusiasm come through to me as well. 'I suppose it's possible, Sue. Alf Brown could easily have been mistaken. The only problem is that we don't know where it is. We have no idea. Presumably all of Shaw's estate was well-documented at his death even if the V & A cabinet had escaped to a convent. Nesfield would be much more difficult to trace. He more or less died in obscurity didn't he?'

. 'Yes, poor man. He married a widow—quite late in life, around fifty—and retired to Brighton. Died three years later.'

The room went quite still and I suddenly heard, clearly, a bus going down the Old Brompton Road two hundred yards away. Sue stared at me. 'What's the matter? You've gone pale.'

'Brighton? Did you say Brighton?'

'Yes.'

'Nesfield died in Brighton? Was buried there?'

'Yes.' She rummaged about in the book, found the page and nodded emphatically. 'Nesfield died in Brighton in 1888, aged fifty-three, after marrying a divorcee, not a widow, called Mary Gwilt, who was an architect's daughter. "A pathetic end for an architect of genius." Why?'

'I forgot to tell you—I ran into Stan Reilly in the car park at Cragside today.'

'Stan Reilly? That rather studious dealer from Hove?'
'Yes.'

Sue closed the book slowly. 'Stan Reilly. He's virtually in Brighton.'

'It may just be a coincidence.'

She shook her head. 'I can see you don't believe that.'

'I have to go to Shoreham tomorrow. Shoreham, Sussex. It's a big timber port now. A couple of miles or so from Brighton and Hove. I think I'd better call on Stan. He virtually admitted he'd never been to Cragside before. Why the sudden interest?'

She jumped to her feet. 'I'm coming with you.'

'You can't! You've your work at the Tate!'

'I'll 'phone them. Tell them I'm ill.'

'You can't! I—I'll be tied up at the timber yards. Nearly all day.'

'I'll wait. In the car.'

'Oh Sue! No!'

'Tim Simpson, have we just agreed on something or haven't we? Either I'm in or I'm out. Permanently. Which is it to be?'

I sighed. I've said that there's no stopping her and I meant it. Even Nobby Roberts has been defeated by Sue's determination and heaven knows how much moral force he can bring to bear. I sometimes wonder, in those tremulous moments that one gets, whether Sue hasn't stayed with me the way she has simply out of a desire for the excitement that my involvement with art sometimes brings. She mostly disagrees with me about the commercial aspects of it all; her view from the Tate is very purist. But then the view from the Tate can be very dull, and Winston Churchill once said that people need change and excitement, otherwise they become bloody-minded. Winston Churchill understood people well and power even better; I had to keep my place with Sue, even at a cost. 'OK,' I said, as firmly as I could. 'You're in. You're crazy and foolhardy and you must promise me to do as I say. Keep close. But I'll take you. If you'll keep close.'

'I will.' She rubbed her hands excitedly together and her eyes, bright and wide, looked hard into mine as she licked her lips. 'Well, well! How super! Since tomorrow is going to be such an interesting day we may as well get to bed early. Unless, that is, you've decided that you're tired after all?'

CHAPTER 8

Shoreham sits on a flat bit of the Sussex coast to the west of Brighton and, on a hard-blowing April day, is just as cold and exposed as Blyth seemed to be, although Geordies would stoutly argue that the English Channel is feeble stuff compared to the North Sea. Whoever is right doesn't matter to me; I had a cold, exposed morning at the port and Sue stayed firmly in the car, reading the papers and accepting the occasional coffee I obtained from various generous sources; port people are hospitable that way. Eventually I had done all I felt I could reasonably do at that stage and I trudged back to the car and got in with great relief.

'Rustington,' Sue said, as I started the engine and boosted the heater.

'Eh?'

'I've made a list. Rustington, not far from here. There's a Shaw house there. Funtington, a bit further on. Stedham, inland a bit: West Dean and Petworth. Or, if you go inland the other way, there's Framfield and Baldslow and Fletching—'

'Sue! Stop it! What on earth are you raving about?'

'Your little habit. Of visiting places that are relevant.

Sussex is liberally studded with Shaw's work. He and Nesfield got a great deal from Sussex and Kent. Would you like
me to—'

'No! Now cut it out! You're mocking me.'

She grinned. 'Don't be so sensitive. If you could poke
around Cragside you could equally well poke around lesser
houses. You never know what you might find. Gothic bookcases in the hallways. Dead librarians in the—'

'Sue! That's in bad taste. Really.'

She pretended to be chastened. 'Sorry. I couldn't help it.
It must come of being with you for a while.

I let in the clutch. 'Well, that's typical. Blame it on me.
I refuse to be diverted. To Hove I said and to Hove I meant.
No digressions, architectural or otherwise.'

Stan Reilly's shop is in one of the Hove streets that is
half-residential, half-commercial, with a few shops grouped
together here and there behind wide pavements under small
trees. There weren't many leaves about yet and the air,
close to the sea, was scrubbed and sharp. I parked nearby
and Sue and I walked back to Stan's shop, on its own at the
end of a brief terrace, so that an access road went down past
the end wall. It was a double-fronted shop with big windows
that descended nearly to the pavement on either side of the
central front door. In one there was a 'Jacobean' oak chest
of drawers with the usual geometric mouldings all over the
drawer-fronts and a brass lamp parked on the top. On the
other side there was a burr walnut piano-top Davenport
and other Victoriana: a bentwood rocker, needlework stool,
workbox in rosewood and so on. I pushed open the door,
clanging the bell, and we went in.

This shop had been Stan's for as long as I could remember
and no one had ever converted the flat above to a self-
contained status because Stan preferred to live over the shop
and be able to walk straight down the staircase into his little
office area, partitioned at the back. There was no workshop

behind the office because Stan always maintained that the presence of sawdust or shavings on the premises, or the smell of hot glue, was bad for customer confidence. He always got his structural repairs done elsewhere by freelance restorers. What there was, however, behind the shop area itself, was another large storeroom, its floor down three steps from the shop due to the slope on which the houses were built. This storeroom was quite big and, because of the slope, much loftier than the shop. Stan kept his unrestored and unpolished pieces there along with items he didn't want to bring out yet or which had been sold and removed from display. Access at the back of the building via double doors made it a convenient point for loading and Stan often used the storage area for cleaning, staining and polishing; the smell of polish was good for customer confidence, he said.

Sue and I moved into the centre of the shop and waited for Stan to emerge. I had a quick look at his display stock and felt a bit disappointed. It was rather run-of-the-mill, nothing exceptional except perhaps for a satin maple sofa table against one wall and a good marine painting of the Pool of London by Dixon above it. Usually, Stan would have something very decorative or exotic to make a splash; the shop was a bit subdued that day.

'Stan?' I opened the office-partition door and called up the stairs. No reply. Shrugging, I beckoned Sue and went to the door to the storage area, plumb centre in the back wall. Beyond the doorway it was darker, shrouded by the squares of furniture, so I felt round the door-jamb and switched on a light without thinking that if Stan had been there the light would have been on already.

'It's a bit empty here, too,' I said out loud, apropos of nothing except that it normally held much more than the stock I could see beyond the three steps down. Neon light-bars flickered and then clicked into a bright glare that revealed a bare space of whitewashed wall at one side, a blank gleam of spotty white brickwork that awaited the arrival of something solid to cover it up. I trod down the three stairs. 'Stan?' I called again, in case he turned out to be in the alley outside, loading up and ignoring the bell-jangle of the front door.

No one answered. Sue followed me down the steps into the storage room with its garish fluorescence of vivid artificial daylight. Polish and white spirit fumes pricked my nostrils with the happy aroma of antique finishers; Stan seemed to have been at work here recently. Stepping round the edge of an oak chest of drawers, I moved towards the large blank space of wall where the smell seemed stronger, and nearly trod on an overturned tin of paint, spreading a dark stain across the floor.

'Tut, tut,' I said, out loud again. 'Clumsy.'

It was blackboard paint. Not black blackboard paint, you understand, but green blackboard paint, the colour of the better class of blackboards, of ping-pong table tops, a satisfy-ing matt sage green like old, old baize cloth. The tin, with its white label printed in red, lay on its side and the paint had ebbed from it across the cement floor.

'*Very* clumsy,' said Sue, her warm soft body pressing up behind me and her dark brown hair brushing the back of my shoulder. 'Look, someone's trodden in it.'

It was true. A dark green footprint, mostly a shoe-sole outline, printed itself across the floor in three fading, reduc-ing marks to the back door out to the alley. I shook my head with a chuckle and walked carefully round the mess to reach the door, throwing it outwards to step across the lintel and out into the service road behind the shop.

There was no one there. No van, nobody loading. Behind me, Stan's big Granada estate stood against the wall, care-fully parked with its nose facing the way out. Behind it straggled the backs of other houses and shops, with oc-casional dustbins against their gates. The sharp April wind blew straight down between the walls, making Sue shiver.

'It's cold,' she complained, 'and there's no one here. Let's go back in.'

We retraced our way back into the storeroom, up the steps, into the main shop display area.

'Stan?'

No answer.

'This is silly,' I said, more to myself than to Sue, and strode through his office partition-wall up the staircase and on to the landing of his flat at the top. Looking back down, I saw Sue halted at the foot of the stairs, her eyes wide as she looked inquiringly up at me. I turned left, towards the front of the building and went into his living-room over the shop, with a big multi-paned window facing south-east that made it very light. He wasn't there either, so that wasn't what made me stop. It was an untidy room, as befitted a solitary dealer-bachelor, littered a bit with papers, comfortably dug into the space in front of the fireplace and the television set, with a big sofa to lounge on. On the sofa there were some books, pulled most probably from the big bookcase on the wall where Stan kept all his reference books, for he was a studious bugger, was Stan, and he had a lot of the classic reference books like Edwards, MacQuoid and Cescinsky. It was the one open on the sofa that stopped me. There was a thick hardback, quarto size, open at the flysheet, across which I could see a familiar legend: *Studies in British Art*. I knew then. I knew, not because that is what is printed by the Paul Mellon Foundation across the flysheets of their books and what is, therefore, printed across the flysheet of Andrew Saint's book on Richard Norman Shaw. I knew because the bookseller, in the manner of old-fashioned booksellers, had stuck his own little monogram-label inside the front cover, facing the flysheet. And I knew I could bet, if I looked inside some of the other art reference books that Stan Reilly had on his shelves, that I would find the same

little monogram-label inside them too, and that like this one
it would say, quite simply:

```
A. Brown. Bookseller.
Hay Yard, Long Acre,
London W.C.2
```

and that the sight of it would make me feel, as I felt now,
overcome by a dreadful fear, a paralysing dose of the willies
that locked me in position, staring at the little label until
Sue's voice from the bottom of the stairs where she had
stopped, perhaps in trepidation herself, sharply called
'Tim?' in a nervous tone and jerked me back to the capability
of movement.

I knew. I knew even though the bedroom was empty
and so was the kitchen. I knew even though, when I had
summoned the courage, I swung open the storeroom door
and found nothing in there but junk. I knew then that the
last room, the bathroom, would contain him and that the
reason the door wouldn't open properly, even though it
wasn't locked, was that the body was slumped against it
from the inside so that I had to steel myself to push it open
enough to peer round into the white-tiled space. Stan Reilly
was there, bundled awkwardly in a heap, limbs doubled
against the pedestal of the lavatory. My guess was that
whoever had strangled him had slipped the belt round
his neck while he was standing having a pee, completely
unawares, and had twisted it tighter and tighter while
Stan struggled and writhed, eyes popping, arms and legs
thrashing, until he was down on the floor and, after that,
until all life had gone.

I went back to the stairhead and leant against the corner

of the landing wall. Sue stared up at me. My legs started to shake.

'The Hove police first,' I said. 'Then I'm afraid we're going to have to upset Nobby Roberts all over again.'

CHAPTER 9

'This is appalling! Appalling!' Jeremy White did a sort of two-step up and down his carpet. 'It is absolutely disgraceful! Irresponsible! You—you—my God, we are due to meet Sir John Coe in minutes and here you are admitting, yes, openly admitting, that you have once again—quite *blandly* I may say—interfered disgracefully in a criminal matter and got yourself further, no, not just further, much *deeper* involved! Hm? Eh? Am I wrong? Geoffrey? Am I wrong?'

Geoffrey Price closed a notebook with a snap and scowled at me before speaking. He's not a bad chap, Geoffrey, quite human for an accountant and loyal to his friends, but he has his weak moments and the Art Fund always brings them out. 'I've always maintained,' he said, with a manner superficially pompous, like a politician asserting a matter of principle, 'that the Art Fund was quite risky enough, quite outside normal investment practices, without adding to it these dreadfully squalid cases that Tim always gets himself into. Without the Art Fund perhaps none of this would happen.'

Jeremy stopped in mid-two-step with a sort of hop and glared at him. Geoffrey had put his foot right in it. 'There's nothing wrong with the Art Fund! Nothing! It has done well!' He gave a glance around him. 'It's just that Tim *always* behaves like a—like a—Jack Russell after a rat on these occasions.'

'Now you're talking like your Uncle Richard.'

Jeremy dropped his fountain pen. I knew my remark would hurt. His office at the Bank is not bad as City offices go but it's not the Chairman's nor is it as grand as the one he'd had at Park Lane in the old days and it didn't have a portrait of the original White, posed in blue coat and white silk breeches in it. There was some panelling, some good carpeting under a respectable mahogany pedestal desk, a long table and chairs for meetings and a window with a view towards Bishopsgate. On one wall hung quite a large painting of Wapping by Whistler himself, depicting the tangle of barges and sailing ships on the curve of the river behind a man and a woman, modelled by Alphonse Legros and Jo Hiffernan, on a balcony in the foreground. Jeremy's glance around him had taken that in and had inferred silently to Geoffrey that the Art Fund had had its successes despite the somewhat murderous events that had brought the Whistler to us and the resistance of his uncle, Sir Richard White, once chairman of the Bank but now departed. On another wall was an earlier painting of a three-masted timber ship en route from Manaos to London which Jeremy had inherited with the office.

'I am *not* talking like Richard!' He picked the pen up with a petulant gesture. 'Although Richard may have had a point, you know, Tim, when he inveighed against your somewhat—somewhat—'

'Tenacious?'

'Precisely. Tenacious qualities. Stubborn qualities.' His face twisted for a moment, darkened, then broke, briefly, into a radiant smile. 'Damn it. Tim! You always do this to me on these occasions! I will not be equated with Uncle Richard. Even if you will continue to attract mayhem. You must accept that as a Director of the Bank, and a member of the main board, I have to warn you that your behaviour is consistently irresponsible in dogging about pursuing criminal leads when you should be getting on with the business!'

'Do you want me to resign?'

'Resign?' A look of absolute horror crossed his face. His voice rose in pitch. 'Resign? Have you gone raving mad? Of course not! Ridiculous! Whoever suggested such a thing? Eh? Geoffrey?' He wheeled towards his accountant.

'Good God no! Absolutely not! Never crossed my mind!'

'Well then!' Jeremy wheeled back to me. 'What on earth are you talking about?'

'Well,' I said, mildly, 'you can hardly expect me to ignore the possibility. I come in here, tell you fully and frankly what has transpired, how these unfortunate and unrelated events have happened, events for which I have had no responsibility, discovered while quite innocently pursuing information in my own time, and what do I get? Dog's abuse. You call me appalling, disgraceful, irresponsible and —what was it—a Jack Russell. Incidentally a Jack Russell terrier is incapable of being bland, which is the other adjective you used.'

'Tim! Don't be flippant, damn it! This is serious.'

'Yes. I'm sorry. But it's quite unfair. The bookseller Brown whom Toby and I discovered was found while on official Art Fund business. I met Stan Reilly while visiting Cragside in my lunch-time. I went to his shop after a missed lunch-hour simply to chat to him.'

'Pah! You admit that the Nesfield connection intrigued you! You always do this!' He gave a dismissive gesture. 'It's no good. I can see it's no good. You'll never learn. All I can hope is that the good name of the Bank will not be impugned in some way. That you'll at least consider your responsibility on that score?'

'Of course, Jeremy. As we always have.'

He flushed, but his eyes twinkled at me. In the old days,

when I started with Jeremy in Park Lane, where he ran a quite separate personal investment brokerage, he would inveigh continually about the Bank, its stuffy and moribund directors, its lack of initiative, its lack of profitability and its stultifying paternalism. As a junior nephew of a cadet branch of the White family his place at the bottom of a pyramidical hierarchy had pressed heavily upon him and his financial freebooting had earned him much pompous censure and patronal reproof. Jeremy's opinion of the Bank then had been expressed with extreme sarcasm and bitter humour. Now, however, he recognized that he would slowly turn into a typical White himself unless someone like me and his charming, shrewd and pretty wife, Mary, once Sir Richard's secretary, kept him from ossifying by stimulating his natural iconoclasm and entrepreneurial flair. He wagged a finger at me and picked up a bunch of papers from his desk.

'To work! To work! No more of Norman Shaw! Coe will be here any minute.'

Geoffrey Price's face was still pained. He gave me a long look of reproof and then got out his own papers so that we could prepare properly for the meeting with Sir John Coe. For some time Geoffrey and I had worked hard to get Jeremy to prepare for meetings properly instead of shooting from the hip, as was natural to him, and it was gradually working. This time he had actually studied the figures and read my reports on the various port facilities and depots, so that when Clara, his secretary, buzzed him that his visitors had arrived, we were all for once satisfied that the others knew their stuff.

There were three visitors. The first to enter was tallish, grey-quiffed, well polished and dressed in a dark grey three-piece pinstripe suit with a striped shirt capped by an old-fashioned stiff white collar. His tie was a red paisley job and his blue eyes were bright under thickish white eyebrows. I remembered his age—sixty-six—from my folder of facts and figures.

Jeremy surged forward. 'John—how are you—may I introduce you—Tim—Geoffrey—Sir John Coe—'

His grasp was very firm. It was immediately clear why he and Jeremy had hit it off. In about twenty years Jeremy would be like this: taller by an inch or two, and fairer, more commanding perhaps, but with the same quick movements, active, well-exercised, clear of speech. The two men behind him wouldn't.

He turned to introduce them. 'Jeremy—our financial director, my nephew, Robert Baker—'

The nephew was in his late forties, quietly dressed in plain dark blue, rather diffident, bespectacled. He and Geoffrey nodded to each other in understanding, chartered account-ant to chartered accountant, professional membership con-veying a mutual experience. He gave me a pleasant handshake and a slight smile.

'My son Peter—our distribution director—Jeremy—Tim Simpson—Geoffrey Price—'

Son Peter was around forty and nothing like his dad except in height. He also wore a pinstripe suit, without a waistcoat, but there the resemblance ended. He was slightly taller for one thing, and thicker, but his movements were nothing like as active and his grasp didn't really try. Brown hair, parted at the side, flowed slightly long over a forehead that had met with little weather to beat it. The complexion was pale and the blue eyes had much less penetration, sliding away a little as he shook hands. Whatever function the directorship of distribution conveyed it occurred to me that it couldn't involve much standing outside watching lorries being loaded with timber. Peter Coe was definitely an indoor man, probably one of your computer-package optimum-distribution calculators, bent over a flickering screen. Sir John was obviously the driving-force.

We settled down to a fairly hefty session which involved each side trying to get the other to come out first and commit itself to some sort of proposal which would give the other an idea of what the first was really thinking. On our side most of it was left to Jeremy, with Geoffrey and I chipping in the odd contribution as we did a sort of tour of the various possibilities we had agreed to explore. After a while it seemed to me that Coe wanted two things: a lump sum of money and the survival of Edwards & Coe in some form that, even if only part of White's timber operation, would ensure the jobs of most of the employees, including his fellow-directors, in service contracts for two or three years. A share swap would be involved and he, Sir John, would stay on the new board for some time but not excessively. I guessed that he wanted to retire and sail; that he had calculated that his fellow-directors were not up to running the business without him; that he wanted to make the best and most responsible deal he could for them before ducking out himself. Understandable and very worthy; the business was in good shape and he was following the admirable principle of quitting while he was ahead.

'Splendid.' At the end of the morning Jeremy was still alert and more enthusiastic than he had shown himself since the start of the affair. 'I'm sure I've got enough to go back to my Board with and we'll take it from there.'

'So have I.' Sir John Coe nodded briskly. 'I'll do the same. Can we fix another meeting now?'

'Certainly.' Jeremy consulted his diary. 'Fairly soon, if possible?'

'Indeed.'

'Oh dear.' Jeremy's face creased. 'It looks a bit difficult next week. Then I have to go to the States.'

Sir John leant back. 'A suggestion: are you going down to the Hamble at all in the next two weekends?'

'Well—let me see—I suppose I could—I—'

'Because for obvious reasons I'd like to keep our meetings as confidential as possible. You'd be very welcome to drop in at Candwell on your way, no, I've got it—why don't you and Mary stay overnight? That's it! At the weekend?' He sat forward again with a slightly apologetic look, as though he'd gone too far, and gesticulated slightly. 'If that's not too —er—pressing for you?'

'No, not at all! In fact it's a very good idea. I'd a plan to go down this month and this'll make Mary concede. Say on Saturday after I've visited the yard? There's some work they're doing that I need to look at.'

'Good! That will suit admirably!' Sir John sat back again. 'Your colleagues are most welcome too, of course. Come for dinner and stay over.'

Three pairs of eyes watched us. Geoffrey shook his head slightly. 'That's kind but I'm sorry: I'm away that weekend.' His eyes met Jeremy's squarely. 'The business you and I have discussed.'

'Oh yes.' Jeremy suddenly nodded at the recollection of whatever it was Geoffrey had been directed to do. His eyes turned to mine. 'Tim. I think that would be a good idea.' It wasn't a request, it was an order; Jeremy needed a henchman. 'Would you bring Sue? Mary hasn't seen her for a while.'

'Your wife is most welcome too, of course.' Sir John's voice was hospitable and he grinned suddenly. 'I can assure you of plenty of room.'

Damn it, I thought, this bloody timber business, I wanted that weekend, but I smiled back. 'Thank you. I'd be de-lighted. So would Sue, I'm sure.'

'Splendid.' Jeremy and Sir John stood up, chorusing together. There was another, final, round of handshakes before Jeremy did the honours in showing them out, leaving Geoffrey Price and myself together. Geoffrey gave me a steady, grey, bespectacled stare.

'Timber talk in a Gothic retreat,' he ground out. 'Please don't take any kindling of any sort along with you, Tim, there's a good fellow?'

CHAPTER 10

'It was Leyswood that did it, really.' Toby Prescott smiled his broad, corner-crooked smile across the table as he forked some more leaf spinach up from the place where it nestled against the veal on his plate.

'Did what?' Nobby Roberts's voice did not actually snap or growl but it wasn't exactly soothing. I gave him a warning glance, which he ignored. So far, my attempt to reconcile him with Toby and to smooth him over about the events in Long Acre and Hove had not been a total failure—he was surprisingly unaggressive—but I hadn't counted it a success yet.

We were in a small Italian restaurant in Covent Garden, not far from Toby's office. It was the sort of place which depends on businessmen because although no individual dish seems to be very expensive, the sum total of your meal always is. So the bill would be mine, not that I objected, because I was the one with the expense account and I was the one, in addition, most wanting to gain from further discussion. Toby had agreed with enthusiasm to meet me for lunch, clearly wanting to overcome the disastrous start at Brown's bookshop, although his voice had hesitated when I had told him that Nobby would be there. Toby obviously still felt great reserve about Nobby, whose attitude was similar, but I knew I had to deal with both until this affair was resolved and I wanted to save time, quite apart from reconciling them to each other.

'Made his name.' Toby spoke round a mouthful of spin-

ach. 'Caused an absolute sensation. It was the turning-point
of his career.'

'I thought you said that Willesley did that,' I objected.

Toby waved a fork in negative vehemence. 'No, no! Willesley was his *first* country house commission. For "Clothes"
Horsley. He got a lot of commissions from artists—RAs—
after that. Lots of them. E. W. Cooke was one, with Glen
Andred at Groombridge. But Leyswood—only half a mile
away—was the decider.'

'Why?' Nobby, for once, showed genuine interest. 'What
was so different about it? It was just another big country
house, wasn't it?'

Toby smiled, another frog-beam of delight at getting
himself an audience, a live audience this time, not just a
printed-page one, and popped another wodge of spinach,
supported by a piece of veal, into his wide mouth.

'Leyswood was built in eighteen-sixty-eight to sixty-nine,'
he said. 'The drawings for it were shown at the Royal
Academy in eighteen-seventy. Every newly successful Eng-
lishman, from Royal Academy painters to Manchester cot-
ton manufacturers, decided that this was just what he
wanted. It was old, it was quaint, it fitted superbly into the
countryside and it looked as though it had grown there over
a period of time. So the fact that it contained a number of
different styles, all old and rustic rather than, say, "modern"
or "new", was no problem. Indeed, it was an advantage.
Think of it; think of our bloody British society. What was
the one thing that a newly-rich Victorian manufacturer
wanted to appear more than anything?'

'Not newly-rich.'

'Precisely, Tim! He wanted to be like the landed gentry.
Even though land was ceasing to be a major source of wealth
and power, to be a country house owner, to have some sort
of ancestry, or to appear to have, was the only way to social
acceptability in this bloody stupid society of ours. You can

trace the whole source of this country's failure to maintain its industrial power, its technological base, to this ridiculous cultural fact. To your English upper class, industry and trade are symbols of gross Philistinism, boring crassness, unmannerly usury, unacceptable. The horse and the country house reign supreme. The country cottage, damp and insanitary, has a much better image than the well-designed, warm, efficient bungalow. The irony of it is that intense Socialists like William Morris fell head-first into it as well. Country was better than town, hand-made better than manufactured, and so on. Unbelievable. Take a look at any fashion magazine now, take a look at the Sloanes, the *Tatler, Country Life.* Horsey women with protruding teeth but without a penny to their name are socially far superior to a computer software manufacturer's pretty daughter.'

I chuckled. 'You've left Leyswood behind somewhere, Toby.'

'No, I haven't! It was built for a shipping magnate. Norman Shaw and Eden Nesfield had hit on a real winner when they brought out the Old English style for country houses. Businessmen flocked to it. Nesfield faded, but Norman Shaw kept right on with it. The list is enormous. The formula was nearly always the same: within commuting distance of their work by the new railways that were springing up all over, but not too near the station to be noisy or vulgar. There were three houses at Groombridge; several at Cranbrook, which is five miles from the Staplehurst station, and so on. You can take it that Norman Shaw virtually invented Stockbroker's Tudor single-handed.'

'That's a bit unfair to him. He was much better than that.'

'Of course he was. Take a look at anything he did. He was brilliant. What I mean is that a whole horde of imitators crowded on to the bandwagon. The country suddenly became stuffed with half-timbered, tile-hung, multi-gabled houses in a sort of mock-vernacular tradition derived from Sussex and Kent. Nesfield and Shaw did that, Shaw more spectacularly perhaps, but the two of them to start with. It was an amazing achievement.'

'Which makes an important piece of furniture by Shaw, or by both of them, so desirable.'

'Indeed.' Toby's smile suddenly faded. 'Even if it does belong to his earlier, Gothic period. Well, perhaps even because of that. How awful this has all become, Tim. I realize that you—well, I hope you won't take this the wrong way—you've had prior experience, so to speak, but I was quite fond of Alf Brown, resentful though he sometimes was. You could always get round that aspect of him and he was a mine of information, really he was, on anything architectural. Now he's gone.'

'I wonder,' I said casually, without any forethought, 'who'll take his place. Someone must be interested in a specialist book business like that.'

'My dear Tim—' Toby's smile returned—'you *have* become the banker and businessman, haven't you? As a matter of fact I rather think that I shall take it over myself. Buy it from his estate.'

I put my knife and fork down in surprise. Nobby gave him a curious, open look of inquiry without speaking.

'You will?'

'Yes.' Toby's face went serious again. 'I've been thinking about it. *The Modern Façade* is a leading architectural magazine. It makes entirely good sense for us to have a specialist bookshop arm which stocks all the great textbooks on architecture and the collectors' items. We get inquiries for them all the time.' His voice gained enthusiasm. 'We could do reprints of out-of-print books that people obviously want. Who better? It would be a fitting memorial to Alf. Brown's Books will live on.'

'Interesting.' Nobby's face was still absolutely open. 'I'm

sure you're right. From what I understand, Brown's clientele
was very extensive and he had a lot of overseas customers,
particularly Americans. His mailing list must be worth
having.'

'Of course. I mean, the business isn't worth a fortune,
you could tell from the way Alf lived, but it's a good specialist
business and, tacked on to my efforts here in Covent Garden,
it would be even better.' Toby's face suddenly gave a spasm
of remorse. 'Look here, this all sounds horribly mercenary
so soon after poor Alf's death, really it does. You must think
that I'm the most frightful vulture.'

'Oh no. It's only natural. You'll have to wait a bit until
matters are cleared up, of course.'

'Ah.' I saw my chance at last; Nobby would have to be
drawn out with care. 'How are—er—matters—going? Any
progress?'

He gave me one of his pursed, recalcitrant looks. 'I long
ago decided that to try and keep you out of things is a waste
of time and effort. You only go poking about and making
matters worse. You and Toby can, I suppose, be trusted to
keep confidences?'

'Really, Nobby! That you need to ask!'

He ignored my indignation. 'As far as Brown's concerned,
the Holborn boys are not having a lot of luck. They've
pieced together his movements for the last few days before
his death and his other contacts. Going through his list of
customers and his mailing list is a massive job. There
are several thousand on it. What we are looking for is a
connection with anyone who contacted him about furniture
of any sort. Now that a connection with this Hove dealer
has been established, *one* of the lines we are working on is
your bloody Norman Shaw bookcase, or whatever it is. The
two things might not be connected, remember. Brown might
have been killed for some other reason and so might Reilly.
Or, one might be the bookcase and the other not. Knowing

your past form, however—' he gave me another very sharp
glance—'it is likely. We've got photographs of the V & A
one and we're circulating the trade. Auctioneers, runners,
everyone.'

'Nothing so far?'

'Nothing so far. I must say it's a very distinctive piece
but it's likely, now, that whoever approached Brown and/
or Reilly will have gone to ground with it.'

'But it must have come from somewhere.'

'Yes. And let us hope that whoever or wherever that was,
someone will come forward. At present, Brown's connection
is very difficult to establish. Reilly is a much better prospect.
The Hove CID are running through all the information
connected with him—his movements, his purchases, contacts and habits. It's a much more straightforward policing
job because we have all his petrol receipts and auction
catalogues, his invoices, all that sort of thing. There's
nothing in the shop that resembles what we're looking for
but the local trade are, for once, being very cooperative. I
believe that we stand a very good chance of detecting the
murderer there. Which I hope will lead us to Brown's killer
too.'

'Good,' I said carefully. 'Don't forget that anyone with
green paint on their shoe must be a suspect.'

He gave me a withering glance. 'Thank you. Most helpful.
All I hope is that you will take no further interest in this
business until we resolve it. I am grateful to you for the
lunch and I do hope that, by keeping you informed, I can
keep you *out* of any further involvement?'

'Yes, Nobby.'

'You'll not try to pursue any further leads of your own?'

'No, Nobby.'

'If anything *does* occur to you, you'll simply inform us and
take no action yourself?'

'Yes, Nobby.'

'That goes for Sue as well?'

'Yes, Nobby.'

'Pah!'

'No, Nobby.'

'God! Give me strength!' He turned to Toby, who had been grinning and giggling throughout, for support. 'I know I can rely on you to keep your distance, but this man is impossible. Impossible. Put up the scent of a work of art for his bloody Fund, thwart him from getting it by some crime or another, and he's off like an Irish foxhound into the bog. Short of arresting him and keeping him locked up, there's nothing to do.'

The conversation degenerated after that so there's not much point in recording it. We finished our lunch pleasantly enough, however, and Nobby shoved off back to Scotland Yard leaving us with a last cup of coffee together as I paid the bill. Toby Prescott was obviously quite well known in this particular hostelry—he had suggested it—which didn't surprise me because he's always been fond of food and the waiter deferred to him in a way that indicated pleasure at dealing with someone knowledgeable. One or two people at other tables had nodded or waved in his direction and it occurred to me that Toby, in his way, must be quite a local celebrity because, apart from being the editor and producer of his magazine, he carried quite a lot of influence. I thought his idea of buying up the late Alf Brown's business was a good one and it pleased me to find someone like Toby thinking in expansionary terms instead of the usual doleful recital you get about how bad things are and how investment will be too difficult. The only thing that interested me idly, in the back of my banker's mind, was how he was going to finance it. After all, he had said very strongly, on the day that we'd first met again, that *The Modern Façade* was great fun but that there was absolutely no money in it.

CHAPTER 11

The drive down to Sussex on a late Saturday afternoon in April was pleasant enough, so by the time we had skirted Horsham I was in a reasonably tolerant frame of mind despite the loss of a valued weekend evening. Sue hummed vaguely to herself in the seat beside me and seemed to be enjoying the ride. Eventually I turned off the main road and we plunged into a wooded section of the countryside, threading our way through the narrow lanes until we turned into the gates of Candwell Park, passing a rather quaint lodge with a steeply-pitched roof and thick white-painted mullions to the windows.

At first, the view of the house was obscured by trees but, quite suddenly, the curve in the drive came out of the thick tangle and Sue gave an exclamation as we got a clear sight of the house. It was large but compact, clustered round a tall tower that ended in a pitched and pointed roof whose eaves beetled out like eyebrows over the windows set in the walls at the top of the tower. The design was derived from the almost-obligatory Gothic of Northern France that so many architects of the 1860s and 1870s felt the need to use but it was lighter, less threatening, and the roofs leading up to it, which piled in a bank around it and sheltered the complex house beneath, were steeply-pitched in a charming, child's-cottage set of angles rather than the massive or ecclesiastical slant of the severe mid-Victorian mansion. Late afternoon sun gave a cheerful light to the building and I felt my heart lift as we came to a halt with a crunch of gravel next to Jeremy's Jaguar saloon near the front door.

Sir John Coe came down the front steps to greet us as befitted the captain of industry playing host in his country seat. He shook my hand firmly, took Sue's with considerable charm and crinkled his active face with pleasure at my appreciative stare upwards, head craned, to look over his roofs.

'Not bad, eh? I understand you and Jeremy actually run your own Art Fund and fancy yourselves as connoisseurs. What do you think? Whose work is it? I can tell you that Jeremy failed the test.' He grinned at us in an amiable challenge.

I gave him a rueful smile. 'Very difficult. If I didn't know better I'd say it might have been Godwin. It's not unlike Beauvale Lodge but it's a bit bigger and it doesn't have that rather French or Belgian half-timbering. Just brick and tile-hanging. The roofs are super. What do you think, Sue?'

'School of Godwin,' she said, firmly. 'Influenced a bit by "Queen Anne" but still hanging on to a touch of Gothic.'

'Bravo! Both of you!' Sir John Coe's pleasure was genuine. 'School of Godwin is right. One of his admirers. Man called Bateman. Didn't do anything much else to speak of. Died youngish.' He put a finger to his nose. 'Fond of the bottle, so the rumour went. But he was a great follower of Godwin's, knew him quite well and consulted him while Godwin was writing all those articles for the *Building News* magazine. In fact, the legend has it that Godwin helped him more than a bit here. Visited the site and advised a few modifications. All those little gables in the roof on the east side?' He put his finger to his nose again. 'Legend also has it that the reason why Godwin was happy to visit the site was that he had a lady friend nearby. Wife of a London man. Building Candwell was good cover for Godwin to be down here.' He gave Sue an open, disarming smile. 'Shocking, I'm afraid. But then Godwin was a bit fond of the ladies generally. It's a weakness one can sympathize with, I think?'

Sue smiled back at him. 'Indeed. I suppose one can. Tell me: have you lived here long?'

'My grandfather bought it shocking cheap just after the First War. The demand had collapsed. Death duties an' all that. It was a bit dilapidated but not too bad in condition. Running it would have been the problem but Grandfather was a bit ahead of his time there. Got the company to buy it, put big timber storage sheds over beyond those far woods to the east and called this the offices. Regional branch, distribution centre; didn't own it personally. Actually, to be fair, the servants wing is in offices but only for local matters. There's an enormous stables and coach-house, quite separate, behind the house; Bateman's client was mad keen on broughams and four-in-hands, that sort of thing, but we don't use it. The clock's been stopped for years. Mostly we're in the house as a weekend place, a sort of flat. And a management training centre or lecture hall.' He smiled a vulpine smile. 'The management being mainly ourselves, of course, although we do have some senior people here from time to time. Seem to get away with it. But come in, come in.'

We followed him up the steps into a large hall with a floor tiled in encaustic patterns and a large marble fireplace. A member of Sir John's staff in a white coat showed us up the wide staircase and we plunged along an upper corridor until he led us into a rather pleasant, dormered room and disappeared, after announcing that the others were having drinks downstairs. Sue looked at the twin beds, smiled a mysterious smile and started hanging up things from her small case in a mahogany wardrobe.

'How's Mrs Simpson?' I demanded, walking to the dormer window.

She put her tongue out at me. 'I've spoken to Mary. She's told the others our real condition.'

'Ahh. How disappointing. I was hoping to get a thrill by posing as a married man.'

'Bad luck. You should call yourself Smith.'

The light was fading and the view from the window was across complex roofs to a dim block with a clock over it. The hands had stopped at quarter to twelve. Evidently Sir John's management training facilities had neglected that particular building and any sense of time's importance for it, but I was pleased to find that he had used the investment allowances connected with business education to install a decent bathroom off our bedroom. I had had uneasy thoughts of Victorian excursions down draughty passages to far-distant ablutions.

We descended to a large high-ceilinged room off the hall where the murmur of voices could be heard over the occasional clink of glass. The same white-coated retainer was acting as barman. He provided Sue with a gin-and-tonic and me with a Glenmorangie while we were hailed by Jeremy with what I thought was evident relief.

The room had a great bay window of full height, disproportionate to the rest of the space, that overlooked a large terraced lawn and distant trees that rose above rhododendron bushes. Facing it was a large fireplace with a complex overmantel and grouped round a fairly dismal fire were Jeremy and Mary, with Sir John Coe and his wife, who was introduced as Ann. Two other couples stood slightly apart, talking together, and I recognized them as Peter Coe and Robert Baker, with their own wives, to whom we were soon introduced. It seemed to me that there was an implied hierarchical grouping in the way they had placed themselves and that I would be needed to engage at the lower level, so I left Sue chatting animatedly to Mary—they've always got on well—and Lady Ann while I grappled with Peter Coe and Robert Baker.

Baker was dry, but pleasant. I found out that he lived outside London at Kingswood, which is in the better Surrey fringes, and doubtless his house was a shrewd investment.

His wife was pleasant too, but noncommittal. Both of them played golf.

Peter Coe was harder to assess; his conversation came and went in bursts of sudden confidences and equally disconcerting reserves of silence or lack of response. His wife had moved off to talk to Sir John's group when I found that they lived in London.

'Well, not London really,' Peter Coe confided. 'Acton Green.' His teeth showed in an apologetic grin. 'Older suburbia.'

'But very convenient now,' I said amiably. 'For the M4 and Heathrow.'

'Under the flightpath, you mean?'

'Why, er, no. It isn't quite, is it?'

'A good deal of the time.' He shrugged. 'Chiswick High Road, Kew, Richmond. They are quite high up—the planes, I mean—but not high enough for me. Or Patricia.'

'But still, for the convenience—'

'My wife hates it.' His voice was suddenly abrupt. 'She's an interior designer. Would prefer something more trendy. She says once you get beyond Earl's Court you're finished.'

'Oh.' I didn't know quite what to say.

'You live in town?'

'Er, yes. Onslow Gardens.'

'Oh well! Patricia will approve of you!'

'But I'm sure you'll have much more space.'

His face lit up. 'That's right. As a matter of fact that's why I like it. We couldn't possibly afford the same house nearer in.'

I was just congratulating myself silently on having said something at last acceptable to this tall, moody man when I felt my elbow being taken. With great aplomb and not the slightest hint of deliberate separation, Jeremy joined our conversation, drew my attention to the darkening garden, pointed out the 'pies' encrusted into the moulded ceiling, moved me closer to a painting by Herkomer on the wall and succeeded in isolating me from everyone else in such a way that we were quite apart together in a far corner of the room. His voice lowered itself to a murmur.

'How thankful I am to see you, dear boy. Sir John is most pressing. Claims he has another Interested Party.'

'What a normal negotiating ploy,' I murmured back, inspecting my nearly-empty glass.

'Yes. He may be telling the truth. But that is not the point. There are complications.'

'Complications?'

'Yes. It appears that the clever grandfather—the one who bought this place, apparently—set the ownership of the company up in such a way as to avoid the dreadful death duties that Lloyd George, or someone like him, set up after the First War.'

'Very wise.'

'At the time, Tim, at the time, maybe. The share owner-ship is, however, complex. Our own Board are going to make a dog's breakfast out of it if we aren't careful.'

'Why?'

'Because acquisition will require a treeful of careful law-yers. The thing is not simply in the hands of the Coe family.'

'Oh.'

'He hasn't gone into this in detail before because he wasn't sure of our real interest.'

'Whereas now he is?'

Jeremy smiled, transferring the smile to the room in general and then back to me again. 'It seems like a good business to me. What about you?'

'So far so good. There are bits we will have to, er, divest ourselves of.'

'As always. Anyway, I thought a word to the wise would be in order. Not too enthusiastic—well, I know you wouldn't show that—but much sucking of teeth, please, when we get to the difficulties of the transfer of ownership.' He gave me a sad look. 'Sir John will be the last of the Coes in this business. I hope it never happens to White's. The others here will be like me when it goes—or at least as I would be now if we sold.' His eyes produced one of his steeliest stares. 'Give it a little more effort and I'll own a *real* share of White's by the time I've finished.' The look vanished. 'With your help, of course, Tim. And Geoffrey's. Shall we rejoin the ladies?'

Quite often Jeremy allows you to forget his real ambition in life but it surfaces frequently enough, like the periscope of a lethal submarine, at moments like these. There are many men who, born into the fringes of a family like White's, are prepared to bask in the name, study the family tree, take pride in their peripheral association. Not so Jeremy: his need for a place in the centre of family affairs is no mere aspiration; it is an intention, a calculation, a purpose, a resolve. The achievement of that objective is an obsession compared to the wild folly of my occasionally obstinate pursuit of an interesting piece of art. It is, I sometimes think, the reason why Jeremy and I understand each other so well. He comprehends very fully that there are certain things in life that you need to finish, even at considerable cost.

We drank another glass before going in to dinner in another high-ceilinged room which I guessed was the original dining-room. This did not have a bay window, which helped to give the walls a better proportional balance. I found, however, that for my taste the ceiling was too high for the floor area, like so many Victorian rooms. Evidently the architect Bateman did not quite have the touch of his admired Godwin and I saw a faint look cross Sue's face as she sat at the other end of the table, where Sir John Coe had carefully placed her within his own ambit. She evidently felt the same disappointment as I did but was too polite to show it; I wondered with amusement whether Sir John had placed her near him after meeting her or whether she had been put there after Mary's doubtless quiet advice on our unmarried status. Sir John might be just old-fashioned enough to be interested in Sue as, conceptually, a mistress.

I found myself between Baker's wife, on my right, and Peter Coe's on my left. Peter Coe was across the table at an angle. It was a good dinner, certainly good enough to invite a man to, on Johnson's dictum, so the conversation flowed easily enough on more or less unprovocative matters. When the table had been cleared Sir John Coe apologized to the ladies, escorted them to the door, explained that none of us was so old-fashioned as to want to remain behind without them in the old style, but that we needed a little time for discussion. They forgave him with considerable charm and left.

I have promised to deal with the timber business briefly. Actually the part we discussed took us about an hour. Some of the points were quite detailed. We even touched briefly on Candwell Park. Earlier, Peter Coe had mentioned that the distribution side was very short of space so I jokingly suggested we open up the coach-house for lorry parking. He replied very shortly that there was no planning permission for use of the house and outbuildings for anything other than office, educational or residential purposes, so I decided that humour was not appreciated or that perhaps he was touchy about the thought of the family losing its erstwhile country seat. That set me off thinking about Toby and his peroration on the English country culture and that in turn led me to thinking how recent most so-called English traditions are; the majority can be traced back no further than Norman Shaw's time. I half-heard, half-missed a monologue by Robert Baker during this train of thought, in which he dealt with some aspects of the family trust's share ownership. I hoped I managed to look sufficiently worried and uneasy to convey the impression that this might be a considerable obstacle. There seemed little point in trying to understand it; lawyers would have to deal with it in conjunction with accountants. I wondered what we would do with Candwell Park if we got it and how, almost certainly, if we wanted to alter it or knock it down, some idiot would make a song and dance about preserving Bateman's work for posterity. Otherwise everything went reasonably well and we rose to join the ladies with Sir John and Jeremy in such good fettle that they told yachting stories for what seemed like hours while we drank brandy.

Eventually we all retired and Sue set herself very primly into one of the twin beds in our dormered room.

'One person, one bed,' she said, smugly. 'Very democratic.'

'Democracy has triumphed over civilization yet again. I think it's been done deliberately.'

'Nonsense! All the rooms are twins. Mary told me.'

'How depressing. Do you realize that at the turn of the century there would have been much coming and going in the passages at night? Now that we all have individual bathrooms there's no excuse. Hygiene has much to answer for.'

'Whose attractions would lure you out into the passages? Into which room would you want to go?'

'This one.'

She smiled with saccharine sweetness as she turned away to sleep. 'In that case you have got your wish. The only difference is that instead of getting one combined arrangement you have got two separate ones. I'm afraid life's often like that, Tim.'

'Only if you want it to be,' I retorted, pulling off a sock. 'Remember what Mark Twain said about a verb: it has a hard time enough in this world when it's all together. It's downright inhuman to split it up.'

'What have verbs got to do with it?' Her voice was muffled as she sank further under the sheet.

'I'm not sure. It just seemed like a good quote to me.'

Sue didn't answer. She didn't need to; as it came about, she was the one who'd been prophetic, not me.

CHAPTER 12

Sunday morning was fine, with a brisk breeze clearing the sky of the few clouds inclined to linger. Our room was cottagey rather than Gothic and the daylight view from the dormer over the back of the big house, across the roofs of the office-servants wing, gave a country-farm impression.

Beyond the steep slated surfaces beneath our window you could see across the weed-strewn courtyard, perhaps sixty yards wide, to the neglected block with its clock-tower poised above another steep roof over a series of high, solid double doors made with diagonal planking. That, obviously, was the unused stable building that Sir John had mentioned, with smaller windows in a pointed row over the big doors. These doubtless gave light to the rooms where the grooms had slept over their charges and the coaches they had assiduously maintained. We take our transport for granted now; all I had to do was to walk out to my XJS and turn a key to give me instant, powerful freedom of movement at colossal speed. The men who built this house and those who had lived in it would have envied me the ability to dispense with the servants, preparation, equipment, bulky fodder and hypochondriacal horses needed to achieve a stately movement through the countryside to the nearest railway station.

The stained glass of the landing windows over the big oak

staircase took the atmosphere quickly back to a guilt-ridden Victorianism as we came down to breakfast. This was served in a high morning-room, also partly glazed with stained glass, so that the morning sun was shot through with blue and red patterns that reminded me that today was Sunday, a day for church and considerations of sin and mortality. The breakfast was cheerful enough, however, with Jeremy hot in discussion on roll-furls and capstans with Sir John, Mary and Sue agreeing with Lady Ann that sailing was a dreadful bore for womenfolk, unless sailors themselves, and myself exchanging minor pleasantries with Robert Baker. Peter Coe came in late, wearing rather muddy brogues which had evidently borne him through wooded walks of an energetic, pre-breakfast kind. He nodded to me affably enough as he helped himself to orange juice, bacon, eggs and coffee. 'I've been pigeon shooting,' he explained. 'Bagged a couple before they all flew off. Are you off too—back up to London this morning?' He drained his juice with a gulp as he asked and set to his plate with a vigour that made his wife, across the table from Lady Ann, raise her eyebrows with amusement.

'I expect so,' I said, glancing across at Jeremy, who was still deep into consideration of genoas with Sir John. 'You too?'

'Oh,' he said carelessly. 'I'm in no hurry to get back. We'll probably enjoy the country for a bit longer. Sussex is a great place for countryside.'

'Yes.' I stared at him for a moment as his words touched a chord. 'Yes. How right you are. Pity to waste it, really.'

'Mmm.' He munched on some toast. 'Stay for lunch if you like.'

'No, that's very kind.' An idea was forming in my mind. 'I'm afraid we have to get on.'

He smiled, a slightly barbed smile that carried a hint of the condescension of the wealthy towards the striving. 'You go-getters. I expect you have to keep up the pressure. Even on Sundays.'

That, I thought, was slightly unnecessary. It revealed just a disturbing existence of aggression. I smiled back blandly: I suppose if your father is selling the family business you can't be expected to like the new owner's bailiffs but I would have preferred to keep matters polite. Looking across at him, however, that Sunday morning, with the particularly Sunday feeling that an old Victorian house can convey, an atmosphere ridden, as I have already indicated, with overtones of guilt and thoughts of duty, I had a sudden desire to leave which was much more powerful than concerns with Peter Coe. Despite the enthusiastic yachting jargon and the bright interest of the ladies in each other, the room brought a profound gloom to me. Work had been finished the night before; I wanted to get out. A sense of claustro-phobia had started, perhaps emanating from an old spirit left from the days when this house conformed to its original, rigid, stifling routine, very heavily, without levity or toler-ance. I gave Coe an impersonal stare, thinking of his remark about Sussex countryside and imagining Toby's cheerful, bulge-eyed face over the Covent Garden lunch-table. Wiping my mouth on a linen napkin, I turned to the ladies near me.

'Sue.' I interrupted their chatter across the table. 'Sorry to have to break it up but you do remember, don't you, that we have to get on? I'll bring our things down and see you in the hall?'

The look of surprise that had come to her face disappeared almost as soon as I'd detected it. She reacted with intelli-gence and loyalty as she caught my eye. 'Oh dear,' she pouted, 'I suppose we must. Just as Mary and Ann and I were really getting started. All right; I'll see you in the hall.'

I left the table with a nod to my host and a smile to my hostess and was back downstairs again, carrying our things, five minutes later. There were formal goodbyes, thanks, a quick word with a slightly consternated—if that is the word —Jeremy that I'd see him tomorrow in the office and then we were in the car, heading for the lodge gates.

'What was all that about?' demanded Sue, smoothing a tweed skirt over her knees. 'I didn't want to go straight back to London. I rather fancied a day in the country.'

'You're going to get one. In Sussex, too.'

'What? Wha—what do you mean? Your face was so set to go I didn't dare inquire. You told Peter Coe you were going back. To London.'

'Yes, well, Peter Coe was getting just a little bit tetchy for some reason best known to himself. He did remind me, though, that Sussex has its attractions and we're going to look at one or two of them. It'll be far better than hanging about at the Coes listening to yacht-talk and being polite to the rest. Business was over last night.'

I drove out of the gates, past the quaint keeper's lodge and turned eastwards. She shook her head sadly. 'Tim Simpson, you are a caution. Where are we going? It's bound to be connected with Gothic bookcases.'

'It's a surprise.'

'Not Hastings? That's your usual haunt when in Sussex?'

'No.'

'Brighton?'

'No.'

'Hove? To Stan Reilly's?'

'*No*. Now look here, Sue, I said it was a surprise, not a guessing-game.'

She ignored me. 'Let me think, now, we're going east. Ha! I know!' She clapped her hands. 'Cranbrook?'

'That's in Kent.'

She pouted. 'We could have lunch at the Willesley Hotel. That's Norman Shaw.'

'No. Sussex I said and Sussex I meant.'

'Tim!'

'Sue! Cranbrook, I mean Willesley, was emptied of all its furniture years ago. It's an hotel.'

'It was his first country house commission. I know it was only really a sort of re-build, an extension job, but it was very comprehensive. It might tell us a lot.'

'I don't think so.'

'Meanie.'

'All right, all right! If we finish what I want I promise we'll try to go to Cranbrook.'

'Give me a clue, then. Where are we going?'

'To the border.'

'The border? Of Kent and Sussex, you mean?'

'Yes.'

She paused, a long pause. I could practically hear her thought-processes grinding.

'Hawkhurst?'

'Hawkhurst? Why?'

She scowled. 'Because it's on the border of Kent and Sussex. Divided right through. And Norman Shaw did quite a lot of work there. Or around there.'

'Wrong. Not a bad guess, but wrong.'

She pouted hard this time. The scowl remained. As I accelerated across yet another back-country crossroads she leant across and pinched, painfully, inside my thigh.

'Ow! Don't do that!'

'Tell me! No wait a minute; I've got it!' Her face cleared. 'Isn't Groombridge on the border?'

'Well done! Yes, it is.'

'Of course. You're behaving to perfect pattern, Tim. As I said at Shoreham. It just took time to guess.'

'No doubt. But see how much better you feel when you find out for yourself. The sense of accomplishment, the— ow! I'll kill you if you do that again!'

She grinned and settled herself back with a contented

smile. Cats are no different; we had one at home that purred as it stuck its claws into your trouser leg.

The cross-country journey took longer than I'd anticipated. It was nearly an hour or so later when we came into Groombridge and, after getting directions from a perambulating churchgoer, we turned by the Victoria Hotel up Corseley Road and went back out into the country again. After a dip into a flat valley containing a pumping station the road rose up from the green meadows back into woods on a rugged hillside and, suddenly, on our left, beyond yet another quaint gatekeeper's lodge, rose the gables of a very large house set back among the trees. Sue let out a low whistle.

'Glen Andred,' she said, having read the sign on the gate. 'My God. Unmistakably Norman Shaw. To think that a painter could afford that.'

I pulled into the side of the road where there was a good view so that we could both have a goggle. There are times when I let myself forget that Sue works at the Tate Gallery and has strong emotions on the subject of art and of painters. She doesn't really like romantic nineteenth-century painting —my Clarkson Stanfield doesn't enthuse her—and I recalled vaguely that Glen Andred was built for E.W. Cooke, who was in the same line of business as Clarkson Stanfield.

'It's enormous,' she said. 'Absolutely enormous. It seems to be divided into two now.'

I stared across at the red-and-white building, lined almost parallel to the road. 'It was after he did Willesley for Horsley, wasn't it? Horsley put him on to E.W. Cooke and from then on Norman Shaw was *the* architect for all the successful RAs. Town and country. Queen Anne style for London and Old English for the country. Cooke had both.'

'But my God, Tim! How many successful RAs in England *now* could afford to have a house like that built for them?'

I nodded soberly. 'Not many. If any at all. Well, there must be some.'

'But Cooke wasn't by any means the biggest name! He was a marine painter, good enough, but not really *great*. Norman Shaw built houses for dozens of them. Luke Fildes, Marcus Stone, Sidney Cooper, Goodall, Webster, Benjamin Williams Leader, Frank Hall and God knows who else. Even Kate Greenaway. Could that many artists afford Shaw houses now?'

I chuckled. 'That was Whistler's fault,' I said.

'Whistler's fault? Why?'

I grinned at her. 'You're the art historian, not me. It's a theory of William Gaunt's. He reckons that Whistler buggered up the art market. At the time we're talking about, RAs were successful members of bourgeois society. They painted, and what they painted was recognizable. Everyone knew what a good painting was and rich men paid big money for it. Then along came Whistler and said absolute crap, you English have no idea about painting, the French are the boys; only the painter himself, or his fellow-painters, know what a good painting is. That did it: if only a painter knows what a good painting is then how can a rich man know what to pay for? Gaunt says you can trace the decline in money paid for contemporary paintings in England from the time of Whistler's Ten o'Clock lectures. Men like those—' I gesticulated at Glen Andred—'could earn thirty or forty thousand a year until Whistler came along. That's the equivalent of a million today. Who earns that now?'

She scowled. 'Whistler! That—that showman. It was Norman Shaw who had to pick up the pieces of the Peacock Room fiasco. And you've reminded me: Nesfield and Whistler.'

'What about them?'

'I read my books over again.' Her eyes met mine. 'There's

an account of Whistler going round to box with Nesfield at Argyll Street in London. At the offices he shared with Norman Shaw. The famous bookcase must have still been there then.'

'So?'

'So maybe Nesfield's was still there too.'

'If he had one. Sue, that still doesn't help us find it.' I put the car back into drive. 'Toby said that Leyswood was the key. Come on, let's go and look at it. It's only half a mile up the road.'

'What's left of it.'

'Mmm?' I gave her a look as the car moved forward.

'There's not much left of it. Just the stable block with its Gothic tower.'

I felt a pang of disappointment. 'Oh well. You never know.'

Indeed you don't. We came to the gates of Leyswood further up the road and I turned in, perhaps impudently, but I was determined to see what I could see; I have this peculiarity about visiting the sites of things, as Sue says.

We were caught completely unprepared. The drive swept through trees carpeted with fresh grass, curved round a bend, emerged from trees below a spectacular rockface and went up a gorge between boulders.

'Stop!' called Sue sharply. 'Look! Oh look, Tim, look!'

I pulled up short and we both stared in delight up to our right where, above a jumbled face of boulders, the remains of the house looked down at us. The top of the Gothic stable-tower was clearly visible back from the edge, peaking high above the superb setting that Shaw and his client had adapted. I realized that, with arrogant confidence, the rocks must have been blasted to make a mini-gorge for the drive to ascend, giving the visitor this spectacular and humbling approach to the house. It was a sensational thing to find in so soft a landscape as Sussex normally provides: Cragside,

Scotland or Wales were the normal associations with this kind of terrain.

I eased the car up the drive, between the rocks, and came to a circular carriage-sweep facing the entrance under the Gothic tower. To our left, a large white-painted gate with decorative canopy was set in a thick bank of evergreen bushes above a flight of brick stairs. To our right was the Gothic tower, with its arched entranceway and the stable block attached to it on the left. Through the arch was a tantalizing view of a courtyard that ended in space. The house, half-timbered and gabled in comfortable Old English prosperity, was missing; our gaze went straight out over the edge of those spectacular mini-cliffs to the wooded rolling beauty of Sussex instead of stopping at the far side of the courtyard which had enchanted the potential customers of 1870. There is, however, something about the work of an architect of genius which always arrests the attention no matter how little remains; even the way the dormer windows were cut into the steep roof above the stables was distinctive, carefully thought out, painstakingly proportioned. It was a brilliant work.

'There's someone living in it,' whispered Sue. 'We ought just to say something or apologize perhaps. We are intruding really, you know, Tim.'

'OK.' I got out of the car, went through the door in a castellated brick wall that enclosed the stable-yard and rang a bell. There was no answer. Whoever inhabited the remains of Shaw's house was out, perhaps fortunately; I beckoned Sue and, feeling like a pair of burglars, we trod carefully under the arch to peep into the draughty remains of a courtyard torn open to the winds by the removal of the welcoming house on the other side.

'It must have been *fabulous*.' Sue spoke very quietly, as though inhabitants or ghosts might overhear us. 'What a shame they had to pull the house down. Even what's left is still absolutely terrific.'

'The billiard-room's there,' I said, looking back to my right. 'Plus the stable-block, the servants' wing on this other side of the courtyard, and the tower. The tower is great.' I walked back up the drive towards the car to take another look at it. 'It's very sort of French-Gothic, isn't it?'

'Yes.' She came back up the drive to join me. 'Very. Actually I think he got it from Nesfield, who'd done it elsewhere. Cloverly Hall.' Her voice became absent. 'They'd both toured Northern France when studying and had drawn all that early French Gothic from building there. This was about his last gesture to mediævalism of that sort. The rest of the houses were Old English, without the Gothic. This was superb, though; a spectacular approach, almost forbidding, a mediæval tower-arch to enter, and then, there across the courtyard, your homely English rustic house with big fireplaces and inglenooks. Very clever. It reminds me a lot of Sissinghurst in its way. The tower is a relic of grim days when big houses had to be fortified against invaders and enemies; the other buildings are timbered or mellow brick, domestic, unchallenging, built in peacetime. The impression is that the place must have grown up over the ages, not that it was, in fact, brand new.'

'Ideal for your rich successful artist or businessman. Amazing. This wasn't for an artist though, was it? Toby mentioned a shipping magnate.'

'James Temple. Shaw's cousin. He was very rich.'

'Really? I thought that Shaw came from a fairly impecunious Scots family.'

'He did. Although his father was from Dublin originally; before setting in Scotland. Died when Shaw was young. The old story: strong Scots Protestant mother, successful sons.'

I smiled. 'The old story. I didn't register Temple somehow; just that he was the client.'

'Dear Tim, how unlike you. You normally store all these biographical details avidly.' She smiled, putting her hand on my arm to reassure me that she was only teasing. 'Didn't you know who Temple was?'

'No.'

Her smile broadened a little and then faded slightly as she turned back to look at the tower. Like that at Cragside, the battlemented parapet was surmounted by a gable-roofed hutch, but this Leyswood version, the original, instead of being romantically half-timbered, was brick-and-tile, very sober, with an almost helmeted side-tower like a sentinel at the corner. Turning back to the car, she took out her handbag, opened it, removed a white pad and got out a pencil.

'What are you doing?' I demanded.

'We haven't got a camera with us. I'm making a sketch of this. Somehow I want to remember it clearly.'

'Well you're the trained artist. Couldn't be better.' I watched her as she started to make quick brisk strokes on the pad. 'You still haven't said who Temple was.'

'Toby was right. Temple was a shipping magnate. As it happened, he became the managing director of the firm Shaw's brother founded.' She frowned up into the light as she turned the pad and put another line into the sketch. 'I don't need to tell you the name of that. Do I?'

I grinned at her, because it was all too easy to answer. These fateful phrases slip from our lips with a facility that astonishes later.

'The Shaw Savill Line,' I said confidently, right there in the spring sunshine with the tower looking down on me like an armoured warrior from a mediæval saga.

CHAPTER 13

'Ships.' I spooned some more marmalade on to my toast, took another swig of tea and pointed across the tangled table-top at Sue with the spoon. 'Ships. This thing has something to do with ships. I feel it in my bones.'

'Look at this mess. The flat is an absolute tip. There's hardly a book in place. The kitchen's full of dirty dinner things. You got up three times last night to check something. I feel absolutely *drained*.'

It was Monday morning and drizzle had started outside, making the whole atmosphere turn grey. The bright spring sunshine of the day before seemed remote. True to my promise, I had taken Sue all the way across to Cranbrook, lunched at Willesley, admired the Japanese pargetting with bottle-ends stuck in it, the peacock and the sheer rashness of a young, unknown architect who could build such a jumble of 'Old English' idiosyncrasy on to what had been a severe, rectangular Georgian farmhouse. There was no original furniture in it or near it. Despite enjoying the trip, the lunch and the view of the house I had felt frustrated.

Long discussion with Sue had followed our return to Onslow
Gardens, gone on through our dinner and long into the
night. Sleep had been impossible. Ideas kept occurring to
me, and dates had to be cross-checked. I felt irritable. Sue
had dressed herself neatly for work again and was looking
suitably subfusc but smart. I was in a City pinstripe that
felt crumpled. Damn it, *I* felt crumpled.

I sighed. 'There's something not right.'

'You've said that rather often.' She helped herself to more
coffee. I drink tea for breakfast, she drinks coffee. Oh,
I've told you that before. Well, that's how I felt; repetitive,
short of ideas, hacking over the same information, need-
ing a breakthrough. Sue looked quite composed for all
her complaint. 'Actually,' she said, 'I think Andrew
Saint says somewhere that Glen Andred and Leyswood
are like ships. Ships on land, a bit rakish, riding above
the landscape like ships over the waves. Cooke was a
marine artist and Temple a shipping magnate. It's a nice
thought.'

'Indeed? It's a nice *fancy* I would rather say.'

'Grumpy! Just because the Robert Shaw theory doesn't
seem to fit.'

'Thanks. I agree. I am. I thought I'd got it with Robert
Shaw. There he was, industrious brother, clever salesman,
winning the business for Willis Gann and they got jealous
of his success. Cut his salary. Typical City bastards. So he
takes his assistant Walter Savill, who is a demon organizer,
with him and founds the Shaw Savill Line. Who better as
a candidate for a magnificent piece of Shaw furniture in his
office? A far better bet than Nesfield, who would have done
his own. I'm sure that the Nesfield theory was a wild goose
chase.'

'Thank you! Very much! It led straight to poor Stan
Reilly!'

'Yes. Well. Sorry. There was that to it, I must admit.

Anyway you were quite keen on the Robert Shaw theory for a while too, weren't you?'

Sue shuffled her cup. 'Yes, I was. Until we found that he'd died of a heart attack. Aged only forty-two.'

'Business risk, poor chap. Anyway he died well before Norman Shaw built the Shaw Savill offices in Leadenhall Street and if he had had a Gothic bookcase or anything like it I think it would have been detected long ago. It must have been a tremendous choice for Norman Shaw. When his brother died in 1864 he was offered the chance of taking his place in the Shaw Savill Line. I mean, Norman Shaw was only just getting started as an architect and he had to take over responsibility for his brother's widow and children. Yet he never hesitated with his refusal. The cousin, James Temple, was already in the business so he took over from Robert and became Savill's partner. Four years later Shaw built him Leyswood.'

'So maybe the bookcase was for Temple. At Leyswood. After all, there's a Gothic tower. Why not a Gothic book-case?'

I rubbed my chin. 'I don't know. Maybe there was. The house was pulled down quite recently: 1955. The V & A bookcase came to light in 1962. We're not getting anywhere. There are too many missing pieces. I must talk to Nobby.'

Sue gave me a look. 'On that note I have to go to work.'

'So do I.'

I put my raincoat on and we departed our different ways, Sue down to the Tate Gallery and me to South Kensington Tube Station and the City. The morning at the Bank was quite uneventfully hard work until, at about eleven, Jeremy burst in.

'Tim! There you are!'

'Been here all morning, Jeremy.'

'Now, now! None of that.' He paced across my bit of carpet-space and plonked himself down in the spare chair.

Like me, Jeremy was back to his City pinstripe but he looked a great deal better groomed than I felt. His blond hair gleamed under the electric light. 'Dreadful weather. Had the best of it yesterday. Talking of which, you pushed off rather smartly after breakfast, didn't you?'

'Did I? Well, Sue and I wanted to get on. You and Sir John were obviously into sailormen's natter so I didn't want to spoil it for you. There wasn't anything more on the business side, was there?'

He eyed me suspiciously. 'You never said you'd be in a hurry to get away when we met on Saturday.'

'Ah no. Just wanted to play it by ear. If we finished, we finished. Question of timing. Would have stayed if the business had demanded it, of course.'

'Ye-es. Pity to rush back to town, though. Lovely day like that.'

'Mmm.'

His gaze became more searching. 'Something special, was it?'

'What?'

'That you had to rush back for?'

'Oh, that. No, not really. Just promised Sue we'd nip back smartly if we could.'

The gaze became accusatory. 'Sue didn't want to come back at all! Mary was certain of that! You're hiding something.'

I struck a dignified pose. 'Really, Jeremy. My Sundays are my own, you know. When business finishes. I really do not have to account for my movements in this Inquisitorial fashion. I—'

'Rubbish! Guilty conscience! You're up to something! What is it?'

'Jeremy, I—I—really—I—'

He slapped his hand flat on my desktop. 'I knew it! I could tell from your face as you left! I know that look. Read you like a book sometimes. You're ferreting again. That cabinet business. Bookcase. Whatever.' He held up a finger. 'Please, Tim. I beg of you. Stay-out-of-trouble-this-time. Got it?'

'Yes, Jeremy.'

'Hopeless. You're hopeless.'

'Yes, Jeremy.'

'To work. It's useless to talk to you. Listen: I've sounded some of the board this morning. The Edwards & Coe thing looks to be on. Subject to certain provisos, conditions and reservations.'

'Naturally.'

'Naturally. Don't look so unenthusiastic. I know I didn't want to get involved at first but it's a good business and it'll fit in with us very well.'

'I have to admit that.'

'Good. Now, the Shoreham operation is important. I want you to go back down there, avoiding Brighton and Hove please, and look into—'

You may stifle a yawn at this point but for those engaged in it, the timber business can be complex, original and challenging. To outsiders it is just a question of moving wood about. Most businesses are the same; talk about business to women and ninety per cent of them glaze over at the eyeball. Talk about businesses to men and ninety per cent of them wait for a gap in your peroration and proceed to tell you all about their own businesses, which induces a mutual glazing of eyeballs. Nevertheless, to those involved there are tremendously stimulatory aspects and Jeremy and I managed to get through an hour before, suddenly realizing he had things to do before attending a luxurious lunch with a firm of brokers, he shot off, leaving me in peace again. I made a telephone call, got my coat and went out, turning through the dull streets with my hands in my pockets. When I got to Leadenhall Street I strolled up and down

thoughtfully before calling a taxi. It's no good looking for
the bright plastered building that Shaw built for the Shaw
Savill Line now; an incendiary bomb did for it in 1941.
When it was put up and its drawings were shown at the
Royal Academy in 1873, it was controversial, like much of
Shaw's London work. It cocked a snook at the dull, respectable business façade of City architecture, for it was a deliberately light-hearted medley of 'Queen Anne' white
ornamental plasterwork, oriel bay windows, square brick
columns, overhanging cornice and other cheerful features
of the late seventeenth and early eighteenth century not
unassociated with mercantile life. From Shaw, Nesfield,
Stevenson and the Morrisian architect Philip Webb we have
inherited a London of cheerful houses in red brick and white
woodwork multiplied by a throng of imitations of 'Queen
Anne' and Pont Street Dutch, but to the conservative City
of the 1870, the offices of the Shaw Savill Line must have
been quite a shock.

My taxi dropped me off opposite Charles the First's
equestrian statue at the south side of Trafalgar Square and
I strolled down Whitehall until turning off into the relieving
cheerfulness of the pub. Nobby was already at a table with
two pints in front of him and, as I approached, a barmaid
sidled up with two large plates of ploughman's lunch.

'Just in time to pay,' he said cheerfully, pushing his sandy
locks back from his eyes. 'Your timing is excellent for once,
Tim.'

'How kind.'

'Thought you'd love to.'

'Such a privilege.'

'Temper, temper. No need to turn nasty. Out of bed the
wrong side this morning?'

'Something like that.'

He gave me a shrewd glance. 'Not losing sleep over
amateur detective work, I hope?'

'No.'

'Thought you were. Sticks out a mile.'

'Bastard.'

He grinned. 'Now you know why policemen seldom laugh. Want to tell your Uncle Nobby everything, do you?'

I drank a lot of my beer and bit into a hefty slab of bread, cheese and pickle. When I had got it down I started talking, telling him about Cragside, Leyswood, Willesley and all the things Sue and I had gone over. He shook his head sadly at the end of my account.

'This is rubbish. Mere vapourings. Not like the old Tim Simpson at all. Idle speculation based on quasi-pseudo-art-historical conjecture. Roaming about Sussex in an æsthetic daze. You say you've even paced up and down Leadenhall Street in a sort of gormless, unfocused sleepwalk? Eh? Good grief, Tim, God knows I don't want you getting involved in a *real* investigation but if you're going to visit Norman Shaw sites for inspiration you'll get arrested for vagrancy by the time you've finished. I mean, look at London alone. You'll be on the corner of Pall Mall and St James, goggling from one corner to the other at the insurance buildings, and then Regent Street quadrant; then you'll be in Chelsea on the Embankment near Tite Street, back to Sloane Street and Queensgate and Kensington and Melbury Road and Hampstead and Albert Mansions, Jesus Christ, before you even *start* on Bedford Park. As for the provinces, the mind boggles. It'll take you to the end of the century.'

I looked at him curiously. 'You've become very know-ledgeable all of a sudden.'

'Well.' He took a draught of beer. 'As it happens, there are one or two lads at the Yard who are quite keen fans. One of the older men worked at Scotland Yard, the old one. Another man was at Kentish Town Police Station. They're both Norman Shaw.'

'I know.'

'Yes, well, there you are. We're not just thick Philistines, you know, despite what you think. And we certainly don't let wild imaginings get in the way of real police work.'

'So you've made an arrest.'

He scowled, pausing with his glass halfway to his mouth. 'Now that's enough of that! If you're going to be like that today, I'm off.'

'Sorry. Let me get you another beer.'

'I should think so.' He handed me his glass. 'It's a touchy subject. We haven't made an arrest. I think we should have. So I've been roped in to being official co-ordinator for the two cases.' He glared at me. 'See what a fine mess you've got me into now, Stanley?'

'Oh dear. Caught between Hove and Holborn, are you? I'll get refills right away.'

When I got back he fiddled about a bit, finished his cheese, crooked his glass in my direction, drank and wiped his mouth with a paper napkin. 'The Reilly murder is straight policework,' he stated. 'I can't think why they haven't sewn it up. We have all Reilly's receipts, auction records, petrol vouchers, cheque stubs, stock books, the lot. We've pieced together where he went and more or less who he saw for the last three weeks of his life. Everyone accounts for their movements.'

'No Gothic bookcase?'

He shook his head. 'Nope. Nothing. He didn't half get about a bit. But there's nothing, no receipt or goods described anything like that. And think of it, Tim; that piece at the Victoria and Albert is enormous, *bloody* enormous. It'd be like shifting a building. No one would miss it.'

I cocked my head on one side. 'Nobby Roberts, I do believe you've actually been to look at it!'

He blushed. 'Of course I have. I do like to know what I'm talking about, you know. We circulated a photograph. Most of the trade fell about laughing. Said if they'd seen anything like that in the last month or two they'd hardly have missed it. You know what I'm beginning to wonder, Tim?'

'What?'

'I'm beginning to wonder if there really was a significant connection between Reilly and Brown. Over this, anyway. Whether the connection isn't just coincidental. And I'm also beginning to wonder whether Brown really had found a Shaw bookcase. If he did, I'll swear it wasn't in the trade anywhere. Not in auctions or shops anyway.'

I bit my lip. 'It might be in a shipper's warehouse somewhere. Hidden from view.'

'That's possible. Just. It would have to have come from a private source, though. A thing like that would never have escaped trade comment.' He stared at his glass. 'Another thing struck me: we've assumed, just assumed, that it's in this country. You realize that that bookseller Brown had an international mailing list? Supposing someone abroad had the bookcase and sent him a photograph? He could have been acting as agent for a foreigner, couldn't he?'

'Yes, he could. Well, I suppose he could. What about the Holborn boys, then? Did they turn up anything like that?'

'No.' His voice was gloomy. 'They didn't. Spent hours combing his office and his papers. Nothing. Not a sausage.'

'Then there's something wrong. Something obvious has been missed. I can't believe that those two murders are unconnected, purely coincidental, and nothing to do with the Gothic piece Brown was trying to sell. It just doesn't make sense.'

'Well, I can't see it. We've done fingerprints, the lot. Some time or another the piece has to come out of the woodwork. I've gone through Toby Prescott's statement about Brown very carefully. Brown said that the piece was a "cabinet or a bookcase, that sort of style". Like Toby's desk. I've been to look at that, too. It's nothing like as

fanciful as the V & A Norman Shaw but you can't mistake
that sort of grim oak semi-religious stuff. Revealed joints
and all that—that—'

'Moral fervour?'

'If that's what you want. Not my description.'

'It doesn't make sense. You've missed something somewhere.'

'Well, all right, Clever Dick, tell me where.' He looked
at me expectantly for once, without the usual guarded
keep-off-the-grass expression that he uses on these rare
occasions, so I felt a twinge of conscience and a real desire
to help.

'Listen, Nobby, it's a long shot but look: Brown's connection is too vague, it could be anyone, but Stan Reilly was a
dealer. Just concentrating on him for a moment, have you
got a full account of his movements for the two or three weeks
before he died? Auctions he attended, shops he visited?'

He nodded hesitantly. 'We've pieced it together, mostly
from receipts. Things he bought. Petrol receipts. It's not
absolutely hour by hour but it's quite good.'

'Was he at auctions much?'

'Seven in that period. He bought quite a few things. Left
bids on some, went personally to some. We've been round
all seven. With a photograph. No luck.'

'Did he pick up all his purchases himself?'

'No. I don't think so. He used carriers for some. Obviously, being a one-man band, he couldn't do it all himself.'

'He'd have needed help for a piece like that.'

'There wasn't one.'

'Damn it, Nobby! This is all wrong! That piece has to
be somewhere and someone has committed murder for it.
Twice.'

'Well, it wasn't in any of those auction rooms. We checked
very thoroughly. They're nearly all provincial; two are South
London but not fine art trade, you know, run-of-the-mill

furnishings. An occasional bit of Victoriana. They'd have wet their knickers over a Gothic bookcase like that.'

'Then the thing has to be somewhere else.'

He gave me a sarcastic smile. 'Brilliant. Where?'

'What will you give me if I tell you?'

'A severe sentence for withholding information from the police.'

I got up, brushing crumbs from my trousers. 'The trouble with you, Nobby, is that you're an ungrateful bugger.'

He did the same, punching me lightly on the arm after he'd swept himself down. 'And the trouble with you, Tim, is that you won't leave matters to the experts.' He gave me a meaning glance. 'Anything that occurs to you—anything —you 'phone me. Right?'

I sighed. 'Right. But I'm thoroughly out of ideas now. Don't expect anything soon.'

CHAPTER 14

I arranged my trip to Shoreham at short notice with Peter Coe's secretary. I couldn't get hold of him personally because she said he was out with one of their vehicles checking on a distribution pattern, which he often did, so I revised my opinion of him as a computer-screen man. Obviously he did real work sometimes. I left a message saying that I'd contact him because I needed some facts on the distribution side. Edwards & Coe were quite large in transport, as you might expect, having bought up one or two haulage companies in their time. To get them, they had had to swallow a couple of removal operations and I didn't really fancy White's going into that, nor did the board of directors, so there were matters to be resolved.

It took quite a time to get through the things Jeremy had

asked me to cover at Shoreham and it was early afternoon when Peter Coe came on the telephone, having got the message from his secretary, and asked rather briefly what I wanted. I explained to him in some detail and he said he didn't have the figures with him because he was in the City, not at his desk, but he could dig them out.

'That's all right,' I said, rather casually. 'I could 'phone you at home later if you don't mind. I've got your address in all the company details—Acton Green somewhere, you said, didn't you? If it's not too much trouble I'll ring you there. If you'll be at home? I have to go back to the Bank now but I meant to check on these removal company operations you own; I'm afraid I've got to get some detail.'

There was a moment's silence, a hesitation, and I thought he was going to be difficult. Then he spoke, his voice a bit muffled. 'That's all right. I tell you what—what time will you be at the Bank?'

'Oh, not before four. I'm staying there a bit late before going on to see a friend in Covent Garden. I won't leave before six.'

'Good. No problem, then. I'll have the figures sent round to you at the Bank in an hour or two's time. You'll have them before you leave.'

'That's very kind. Many thanks.'

'No sweat. Anything else?'

'No, thanks.'

Efficient fellow. Doubtless he guessed that White's were anxious not to buy themselves too deeply into ramifications of his father's empire which spread beyond timber and the hauling of it. What quite we aimed to do with the businesses, if acquired, was another matter.

I finished at Shoreham and dutifully skirted round the north of Brighton and Hove, avoiding them as Jeremy had instructed. In no time I was on the A23 and then the

motorway, the M23, heading for London. You know how it
is on motorways: you blaze along for a while and then you
get bored, so you start to notice the commercial traffic in
front of you, the lorries and the vans, with their company
names, companies you've dealt with or been associated
with or whose products you eat, wear or drink. I'd passed
Gatwick and was racing northward when a big removal van
came up ahead, washing along in the light April drizzle.
Pavilion Removals it said, right across the back of the
pantechnicon doors, London and Brighton, Weekly Service.
Telephone numbers in London and Brighton were marked
underneath, visible above the spray from its back
wheels.

Well, well, I thought, small world, that's one of the
removers that is a subsidiary of one of Edwards & Coe's
haulage companies, I remember from the files. Not a bad
outfit by the accounts. I was overhauling it fast. A standard
weekly run and a bookable special service for moving house
or other needs. The huge side of the vehicle came into
view, repeating the great Pavilion Removals' legend and the
telephone numbers with a bit more detail on the street
address in Brighton and a depot in London's Turnham
Green.

Turnham Green. For a moment I nearly threw a wobbly
on the wet road surface. Nobby had said I was wasting my
time in capering or vapouring about at Norman Shaw sites.
But I'm superstitious, and if ever there was a pointed
reminder this must have been it. Only a strong sense of duty
persuaded me to fulfil my obligation to return to the Bank
and go on to visit the offices of *The Modern Façade* afterwards;
when you get a pointer like that you feel you must follow it
up immediately, in case it vanishes or your mind slips it,
out into a bit of the memory-bank that doesn't have a recall
system. I trembled on the verge of turning off to the west
when I came into the outer tangle of south London but

then duty called, and it was raining, so I steered my way obediently to the City.

As it happened, I worked very hard once I got to my office because there were corners I couldn't cut and the figures Peter Coe had sent needed more than a glance, so I was a bit late leaving. I got to Toby's office just as the staff were abandoning the place in that casual way that magazine and media staff in London have of drifting out towards pubs and boyfriends and home. There was a cheerful litter of the same paste-ups, art posters, heaps of paper and smart weeklies or monthlies that I had seen before. Toby came out and greeted me himself because the snooty receptionist had gone, leaving her rubber plant and the coffee table fanned with the coloured copies of *The Modern Façade* in such careful arrangement behind her. I traipsed after him into his office, refused a drink and accepted coffee before sitting down on the rush-seated corner chair with the sweeping cabriole leg at the front.

'My goodness!' His face looked concerned behind the bantering front he always puts up. 'You do look glum! What on earth's the matter?'

I sighed. 'There's something wrong about this whole Norman Shaw business. Something doesn't fit.'

'What?'

I couldn't put my finger on it. I tried to explain to Toby, peering at him across the panelled back of his desk in an unfocused way that took in the careful Gothic edge moulding without caring to register it closely. I explained to him how far things had got, or rather had not got, and he beamed and said I was incorrigible but if it would help we could talk it through because, apart from Alf, whom he'd liked and known well, the whole question of the missing Shaw piece was making him lose a lot of sleep, too. It was after some time that I suddenly couldn't hold back any more and said that I had this funny feeling that the thing was somehow connected with ships or shipowners.

'Ships? Of course!' His face bulged at me across the desk-top. 'You should have asked me: I'd have told you straight away.' He waved a hand at the shelf-covered wall, lined with books. 'It's all in there, Tim. Yes, dear, yes, I'll lock up.'

The offices of *The Modern Façade* had been steadily emptying and, from time to time, a different female face would appear round the door and say good night, she'd put her lights out and would Toby please lock up and he'd say yes, yes, like that, impatiently, and we'd go on talking and drinking coffee from a big red percolator-jug he had plugged in to a socket at the side of the Gothic desk. He had a shirt with broad blue-and-white stripes under a white collar this time, and a startlingly electric-blue tie with white polka dots. The suit looked like the same one as before: a grainy, slightly coarsely-woven grey, almost hopsack cloth that gave a deliberately textural effect such as only an architect would insist upon, as though to make sure that you knew that his suit was made of cloth and not something else, something artificial and smooth and perhaps plastic.

'An association with the sea and ships can never be separated from Richard Norman Shaw,' he repeated. 'Look at his major private clients, the really big ones. Three out of four of the great newly-rich ones were shipping men.'

'Really? Who are you talking about?'

He smiled happily and began ticking them off on his fingers. Like so many editors, journalists and publishers, Toby was something of an evangelist, a compulsive lecturer and preacher. Direct opportunity made him happy. 'One —your Leyswood man, James Temple. From him came not only Leyswood but warehouses and the Shaw Savill Line offices. I know he was a cousin but he kept up the shipping connection. In fact it was no accident that number two,

Ismay of the White Star Line, provided ships and crew for the Shaw Savill Line when they got into financial difficulties in the 'eighties. Shaw built Dawpool for him; he died long before the *Titanic* disaster. Then there was Leyland of the Bibby Line; another Liverpudleian, like Ismay. He was one of the grandest. Shaw could deal with him better than most —he was difficult—and picked up the pieces at Princes Gate when Leyland and Whistler parted brass rags over the famous Peacock Room. Shaw was amazing that way; quiet and unostentatious and Scots, but a magnetic personality. He had no trouble with rich clients and could handle them all with confidence.'

He stopped and topped up my coffee. 'Shipping tycoons seem to have been able to make money quickly. Those three men were all in their forties when they became rich.'

'You said three out of four. Who was the odd man out?'

'Your own Armstrong of Cragside. He was in armaments, as you know. And older. Shaw got him through a contract with Horsley at Cranbrook. Armstrong's wife saw the work there.'

I shook my head. 'Somehow I keep ruling Cragside out. I've got this thing about ships.'

'Really, Tim, you are a funny fellow! You're not psychic or clairvoyant are you? You? One of the most practical, the most—er—most prudent sorts of men?'

'I think that the Shaw Savill connection—which was his earliest really maritime client—was important to him. I think he might have designed a splendid piece of furniture for Temple.'

Toby's face puckered. 'I doubt if it was at Leyswood. You think it was at the offices? New Zealand Chambers in Leadenhall Street? Impossible to find out, I'd say. The partners—Savill and Temple—shared an office there, a big semi-circular office specially designed for them. All bombed out in the war. Dead end. More coffee?'

I got up. 'God, no. I'm bursting already. Where are your loos?'

'Loo. The loo. My loo is just across the hall. I *hate* sharing loos with my staff. *You* are welcome to use it.'

'How discriminatory. And how kind.'

The hall light was not particularly strong and the rest of the offices were in darkness. The desk behind which the condescending receptionist normally sat was empty. Toby's own personal toilet facilities were beyond a door to the left of the entrance and comprised a cubicle with the usual pedestal and a tiny washbasin with a blue-and-white hand towel which would have matched his current shirt perfectly. Not that I was terribly interested at that moment; I simply stepped inside quickly, only half-closing the door because we were alone, and got on with the business I needed to do so urgently.

It was a hell of a relief. Such a relief that, when I had finished, I was quite oblivious of anything except zipping myself up again. So that when the swing of the door fanned a movement of air on to the back of my neck I didn't really bother and, in any case, it had been a long day what with driving down to Shoreham and back, getting to the Bank, looking at figures and now trampling all over the same ground again with Toby, trying to speculate—

The band constricted my neck so suddenly that my head jerked up in an astonished rigor of stiffened reflex. The material bit deep into my flesh, throttling my windpipe. It was like being hanged, but more slowly. In immediate reaction I made the classic mistake of whipping both hands up to grab the noose, too late. I couldn't get my fingers between it and my flesh to obtain a relieving purchase. There was a great thrust into my behind and I realized that the assassin had driven a knee into it so as to brace me backwards, taking the purchase off my feet. My lungs expanded without achieving any inhalation at all: a tightness squeezed my chest. My eyes began to bulge as darkness fringed the edge of my vision. Silver spots started to coalesce into big patches as the throttle tightened from excruciating to terminal. I let out a great half-croak, bitten off by lack of air.

Now the noose was being twisted at the back of my neck to bite in deeper. I tried a backwards head-butt in stupid desperation, only making things worse by giving a better purchase to the binding, squeezing, contracting strangle-band. A blinding intelligence came to me that this was *it*, finish, all over unless I did something really drastic in the next few seconds before, taken completely by surprise, I lost consciousness. How stupid, I thought, I haven't used my arms yet or my legs, I've been a classic victim, pulled backwards off balance and next thing down I'll go to the floor and that will be it.

There was obviously only one way to go: backwards. I put one foot up on to the lavatory basin-edge and found, with my left hand, Toby's dinky little washbasin. Then I drove backwards with those purchases and all the muscle I could muster.

Partial success. There was a great slam and grunt as I rammed backwards into my attacker and, locked together, we hit the door-post. Even better, as the solid upright stopped us I jerked my head back in a last desperate back-butt and connected hard, very hard, with a skull behind me that was already stopped short against the jamb. I heard a great crack and a gasping grunt, the noise of someone badly hurt, as bright stars flashed among the silver patches and blackness that had now taken over my vision. Over-balancing, I went down backwards on to the lavatory floor, hearing vague noises of distress as I collapsed into semi-consciousness, grasping now at the murderous binder round my throat.

I got a purchase on it and pulled, my head jammed

against the wall under the washbasin. Just when the last black-pressured agonized moment seemed about to arrive there was a tight rush of air as the noose slipped out an inch. The pressure dropped. With a painful whistling I got a merciful gust down into the system. Then, as I pulled, the band round my neck, twisted at the back, slackened and gave way completely, leaving me heaving, gasping, choking and coughing on the tiled floor of Toby's personal blue-and-white loo.

I don't know how long I was there. It might have been several minutes or it might have been tens of seconds. All I know is that it took much longer to get back my vision than I would have liked and I went on gasping and heaving and croaking until, intelligence returning, I managed to pull myself up via the wash-basin and sit, bent double, on the lavatory basin I had so recently used with gratitude. Then I managed a lot of deep breaths, which got my oxygen back towards normal and my whole, racked physique back to a more acceptable level of discomfort. Boiling with rage, I lurched out of the cubicle and into the hall, looking for someone to murder. I found I was holding a paisley-pattern tie in my hand, clutching its twisted material from where I had freed it from my neck.

Toby's black-polished shoes came into my vision first. They were right outside the door, pointing upwards. The rest of Toby was stretched out beyond them, flat on its back. As I moved quickly forward to kneel beside him I saw the blood on his forehead where a great gashed contusion marked the blow that had laid him out. I didn't try to move him; I went straight to a telephone. I didn't see the other contusion on the back of his head where, apparently, he must have hit the receptionist's neatly magazine-stacked coffee table as he went down. They told me about that much later.

CHAPTER 15

The police arrived before the ambulance. The two uniformed coppers took a careful look at Toby, asked me a few questions where I sat, still half-throttled, and made notes until the ambulance men arrived and carried him carefully off on a stretcher. I gave the policemen more information, told them to contact Holborn and Nobby Roberts if they could, and repeated what had happened for the fourth time. They seemed to have difficulty believing me but, as I got fairly emotional and demanded that a doctor look at me too, they relented and took me with them in the car they'd left outside. It all seemed to take ages.

One of the policemen sat with me as I waited in casualty and then, as more people came and went, I began to get news of Toby's condition. Apparently he did not have the same thick skull structure that I have and the head-bashing he'd received had cracked his, rendering him deeply unconscious even if not actually in a coma. As time went by Nobby arrived with a Holborn CID man, all irritation and lack of sympathy for my painful neck. They pushed me to one side and went off into the inner depths of the hospital but they couldn't get anything out of Toby at all, just very vague responses and murmurs, not even a recollection of my visit, let alone the attack. The doctor got angry with Nobby for pressing the point and shooed him out. Nobby got very stroppy and said that not only was he a senior police officer but he was a personal friend of a senior physician at the hospital with whom he'd played rugger, and the young doctor then grinned and said he played rugger too, so what? Then Nobby and the CID man left, taking me with them, after making arrangements for a policeman to wait at the hospital until Toby improved. We went back to Covent Garden, to the offices of *The Modern Façade*, and I described the whole thing as best I could and they looked at each other significantly before calling a forensic specialist who started to take scrapings and samples off the door-jamb and everywhere else that mattered and didn't matter, it seemed to me.

I sat down in a chair in reception and watched them. The back of my head was bruised and tender but it was my neck that was the real trouble. It was bloody painful; very stiff and extremely sore. My breathing still seemed to be impaired. They had taken a look at me in the hospital and murmured a few condolences before announcing that there was nothing wrong, nothing that a few days wouldn't improve, that is, and made light-heartedly impudent remarks about the thickness of my neck, which annoyed me. Nobby wasn't much better: he kept looking at the paisley-pattern tie, now in a polythene bag, and asking me whether I'd ever seen it before and I answered for the umpteenth time that I hadn't, it was just an ordinary mass-produced tie of the sort you see everywhere. No one I'd been in contact with recently had one like it. I even thought of Sir John Coe, but his was a different colour. Toby, of course, had been wearing his blue polka-dot job which was just as well for him because Nobby and the CID man were fairly clearly marking him down as suspect number one in their minds, despite unbelieving protests from me.

'You were alone in the office with Prescott just before it happened?' the CID man demanded.

'Yes, but—'

'You didn't see or hear anyone else in the office?'

'No. No I didn't, but—'

'You've said you have no idea who came up behind you? Didn't see him at all?'

'No.'

'He didn't say anything or make any sound that you recognized?'

'No.'

'Just walked in behind you and slipped the tie round your neck?'

'Yes.'

'Must have been about the same height as you, or taller, and pretty strong.'

'I suppose so.'

'Funny that he knew exactly where you were. In this manager-only toilet.'

'Well, he might have seen me go in. If he was hiding in the office somewhere.'

'Mm. Prescott's about your height.'

'Yes, yes, I know, but—'

'You banged your head backwards into your attacker *after* you'd driven him up against the door-jamb. He can be expected to have a contusion of some sort somewhere on the front of his head and on the back.'

'I suppose so.'

'Prescott has both.'

'But that's from the table in here. The back one, I mean.'

'Possibly, sir. Forensic will have to establish that. With any luck there'll be hairs on the door-jamb although it's not a certainty.'

'And on the coffee table here.'

'If that has been involved too, then yes, there may be. Again, it's not a certainty.'

'No.' I felt very glum. It was inconceivable to me that Toby could have been my attacker. If he really was involved in this whole affair criminally, why wait until I was on his premises before trying such a thing? And though Toby was not weak physically, he knew from college days that an ex-rugger Blue, a front-row scrummager, is not a man you attack lightly, even if you do have the advantages of surprise

and rear purchase. He would have to have been desperate.
I racked my brains in going over our conversation that
evening, what I'd said and what he'd said. All of it came
back to my conviction about the shipping connection and
the Shaw Savill possibility: was there something I'd said
about that or the possibility of the Gothic bookcase being
made for Temple that had sparked something off?

Nobby drove me home and abandoned me on the door-
step, very late. He wouldn't answer questions and he just
grunted at most of the half-speculations I threw at him. It
made me very cross. I couldn't argue with the line he was
taking: that this attack would have to be treated on its
own merits and its evidence sifted for conclusions quite
independently of the other attacks, on Brown and Reilly.
Each new attack opened up its own line of evidence, adding
to the total in a way that would help to solve all three
perhaps, but only perhaps. I began to realize that Nobby
was holding back a bit in sympathy for me because he knew
that I liked Toby enormously and his own suspicions would
upset me. That irritated me, too. The only consolation was
that Nobby seemed to have taken over his co-ordination
role with great seriousness. He let slip that he had the
complete file on the Reilly murder with him at his office, so
he was evidently trying to do better than the Hove crowd
had managed to do so far. I said good night to him feeling
a bit happier in the knowledge that Nobby was getting
deeper into things himself.

Sue was waiting up for me. I'd phoned her from the
hospital and told her, very approximately, what had happened, emphasizing the danger to Toby rather than myself,
but she was still extremely edgy.

'Oh Tim! Look at your neck!'

She grabbed me very tightly and, gratified, I put my arms
round her and made soothing noises. I was immensely
grateful to see her in a way I couldn't properly express, so

I just held her and kissed her while she demanded to know everything that had happened, everything in every detail. After a while I steered her to the sofa and told her the whole story, which seemed simple enough in the re-telling. Her eyes were wide.

'Do you think it was Toby?' she demanded.

'I can't believe it.'

'Why not?'

'It doesn't make sense. Think about it. If Toby wanted the piece, why approach me in the first place? Why not tell Alf Brown he would have it himself? Or Stan Reilly. Or whoever. Unless he changed his mind after contacting me. But why attack me right there at *The Modern Façade*? What would he have done with my body?'

'Dumped it,' she said, promptly, and with a conviction I didn't like.

'Alone? Without help?'

'It's possible.'

'Possible, but not probable.'

'Nobby and his lot seem to think so, from what you've said.'

'Yes, I think they do. I simply can't accept it. I can't believe that my conversation with Toby could have suddenly made him so desperate.'

'Tell me again. Come on: everything you discussed.'

With a sigh, I went over it all again, sitting on the sofa holding her hand with the big Clarkson Stanfield marine painting looking down at us. When I got to my remarks about the shipping connection a troubled look came into her eyes.

'What's up?'

'It—it's a strange coincidence, in a way.'

'What is?'

'The shipping connection. I've a confession to make. I had to go to the Westminster Library today. To look up a reference in the art section. Nothing to do with Norman Shaw.'

'So?'

'So on my way back down I passed the general section and I couldn't resist going in to look up anything they had on Shaw—the brother, I mean—just in case, you know, just in case there was anything, anything at all. It was visiting Leyswood that did it.'

I chuckled, which was painful, but still. 'Sue, you are incorrigible. You're getting worse than me.'

'No, I'm not—it's just your influence. Anyway I couldn't find anything on him or on Temple but I did find a book on those emigrant ships to New Zealand that covered all the trade in the early days. There was quite a bit about the Shaw Savill ships in it.'

'Really? Anything relevant?'

Sue shook her head and then, still holding my hand, she told me about the bad luck the Line had had in those early, perilous days, about the dreadful fate of the *Cospatrick* and then the *Merope*, the *Caribou* and the others that were wrecked or in collision or simply disappeared. She had noted down the names and she told me the story simply and factually, which somehow made it seem all the more stark and horrifying and so remote from the grand houses, the celebrated furnishings and the art collections of the men who had remained on land to finance and organize the dangerous reality of life at sea in the nineteenth century. There was a long silence when she'd finished because somehow I felt even more strongly, now, the inexplicable pull of the shipping connection with what had been going on.

'Keep your notes,' I said, getting to my feet. 'With any luck Toby will return to consciousness tomorrow and this whole thing will be cleared up, especially if he recognized the attacker. So we may not need them. Whatever happens, though, there's one last place I have to go to, one last location

to check. I know that Nobby says I've been wandering about
vapidly but I do get more information clear in my head, a
better picture, when I visit these places.'

She looked up at me from the sofa with a smile. 'Dear
Tim, where on earth do you want to chase to now? Still in
hot pursuit, just like a terrier? I'm coming with you, you
know, so you'd better tell me. Where is it?'

I reached down and lifted her up off the sofa to stand in
front of me so that I could put my arm around her waist.
'It's very intellectual,' I said. 'We're going to Turnham
Green.'

CHAPTER 16

'William de Morgan tiles,' I pointed out, raising a pint glass
in their direction. 'Never thought I'd be so glad to see such
things again. Not that I don't admire William de Morgan's
ceramics, I do, but somehow I never thought I'd view them
with gratitude, if you follow my drift.'

'I suppose I do,' she said, looking first at me and then
down at her hands, quickly.

We were in the Tabard Inn, Bedford Park. Just round
the corner from Turnham Green station, West London, that
is. You can see it from the Underground train going out to
Heathrow if you want to, because the Underground goes
Overground at that point, in fact it's elevated well above
ground level and I'm rambling, aren't I, but I was feeling
somewhat light-headed that morning. Waking up with a
much less painful neck had helped, and having Sue beside
me, and the spring sunshine. It made me feel decisive and
dynamic. I had checked with the hospital: no change in
Toby yet, but hopeful signs. I left a message at the Bank,

avoiding Jeremy and Geoffrey, recovered my car and took
Sue, late morning, over to see what was probably the first
Garden City suburb in the world. Bedford Park was laid
out by a man called Jonathan Carr and mostly architected
by Richard Norman Shaw, although E.W. Godwin managed
to get a couple of houses in at the beginning. There's still a
good deal of it left because a plan the local borough had,
after the 1939–45 war, to raze it to the ground and build
council houses over it was shelved. Bedford Park survived;
its leafy roads still contain most of the original brick-and-tile
houses, with their white-painted balcony balustrades, their
little Dutch gables, oriel window-bays and other cheerful
'Queen Anne' features.

I had driven Sue carefully down the principal roads: The
Avenue, Woodstock Road and, finally, Bath Road, where
we came across the celebrated pub called the Tabard Inn,
which Shaw placed across the road from the church, facing
it and even rivalling it, because the Inn building included
a stores and club all under one long roof, with seven gables
aimed at the street. The pub is at the end and the sight of
it had made me thirsty, so I parked nearby and took Sue
in. Although the William de Morgan tiles are still present,
there have been changes; for one thing the walls have been
re-papered in a William Morris print, which would have
made Shaw writhe, particularly since it is a design that you
see on so many settees nowadays. Alcoves contain cubicled
bench seats with tapering oak Voyseyesque uprights in an
Arts-and-Crafts manner and a 'Morrisian' patterned carpet.
The front ceilings are still heavily moulded, however, in
their original Renaissance design and, despite the bloody
jukebox and the wretched fruit machine, the multi-paned
windows in the doors, with their ovals and heavy, painted
glazing bars of 'Queen Anne' style remind you of what the
original must have been like. That, the sunshine and the
relief of feeling that my neck actually worked again counter-

balanced any loss of expectation that the interior of the Tabard Inn might have caused.

Sue gave me one of her looks, the ones that convey the sense of my incorrigible nature, over her glass of white wine. 'Well? Now that we are on site, so to speak, what conclusion have you come to? That the bookcase went for six when they pulled Tower House down? Or that it's standing in the church vestry opposite and all we have to do is hire a gang of removal men, pretend we've been sent by the Commissioners to take it for restoration and off we go?' Her smile mocked me.

'Church vestry,' I said. 'That's a thought. I doubt if it's there but we could look. As for removal men—it was seeing the Pavilion Removals van that reminded me of this place. Their depot is here somewhere.'

She shook her head in mock sadness. 'I think that Jeremy and Nobby are right. You're hopeless; you can't resist prowling about like this, sniffing for inspiration. You really should leave professional police work to professional policemen and forensic science.'

'They take too long. Besides,' I said, indignantly, 'what about you? Raking through out-of-print books on sailing clippers in the Westminster Reference Library? Hey? All that esoteric stuff about the *Cospatrick* and the dreadful *Yarn of the Nancy Bell* type of story? What is that but hopeless sniffing for inspiration?'

Her chin lifted. 'Well, it's been as much use as your researches go as far as finding this enormous piece of furniture is concerned. I may have nothing to show but nor have you, either.'

'Ouch.'

'I try to help you with your intuition about shipping and all you do is to deride my efforts. *Yarn of the Nancy Bell* indeed. The only Gilbertian aspect of this affair is the sight of you, going round in circles.'

I gave her a significant stare. 'Don't be too sure of that. Quite apart from writing *"I am a cook and a captain bold, and the mate of the Nancy brig, and a bo'sun tight and a midshipmite and the crew of the captain's gig—"'*

'Stop it!' She shivered. 'That's a horrible rhyme for me, now. Horrible. Gilbert had a macabre sense of humour. He—'

'He did indeed. He re-named his big house in Harrow Weald. He called it Grim's Dyke. Its original name was Graeme's Dyke. Guess who built it?'

She stared at me. 'Of course. Richard Norman Shaw.' Another shiver made her tremble.

'Right first time. Smack on. For Frederick Goodall, actually. The Royal Academician. I seem to recall that Hesketh Pearson called it a "sham Tudor" house. Shaw might have had a few words to say on that. Anyway Gilbert bought it later on, in the 'nineties. So who knows—Gilbert may come into things yet.'

'Tim, you don't think that—that Gilbert got *The Yarn of the Nancy Bell* from reading about the *Cospatrick*? Do you?'

I shook my head. 'Don't think so. I think the Nancy Bell was written in the 'sixties, well before the *Cospatrick*. But it was rather strong meat: *Punch* turned it down.' I gave her hand a reassuring pat before lifting my glass for a soothing draught, and, carelessly looking up, got a view through the Inn window of the Gothic-arched stone mullions of the church opposite. I put the glass down thoughtfully. 'In the meantime, before we decide that *HMS Pinafore* or *The Pirates of Penzance* are the key to all this, let us follow up that suggestion of yours about the vestry and look over the church. I have a thing about looking around churches, as you know. Not for ecclesiastical reasons, of course; just the odd biographical curiosity at work. What was it? "If only because so many dead people lie around"?'

She frowned. I put my arm around her for a comforting

squeeze and we came out of the pub to face the church, opposite. St Michael and All Angels, Bedford Park, is an odd building, combining Gothic features with the 'Queen Anne' bits and pieces of the surrounding development in a low-key manner. That these features are derived from the Renaissance is merely a matter for purists. There is a long roof above the old red-brick body of the church and this roof has been re-tiled fairly recently in hard, livid-red shiny tiles which set the teeth on edge; they have no relation to the old tiles or to the mellow brick beneath. Cut into this roof are the three dormer windows of the clerestory, deep set in their stone arching and shaped in that 'Dutch' manner of the English Renaissance. Above the roof is a four-columned white bell-cupola that looks like one of the small belvederes that Shaw liked; the effect is somehow slightly Chapel rather than Church. Certainly it is not a Victorian church in the way that I have come to think of Victorian churches, all tension, high-notes and encrusted stone. It is much more like the Lutheran churches of Scandinavia or the cool simplicity of Wren, where the rational human being can worship without the attitudinizing that Victorian Gothic seemed to demand.

There was a green-painted notice-board outside, with white lettering, giving the usual information about services and the vicar. We strolled past it, into the slightly ponderous porch and then into the church via a door on the left. The first thing that hit my eyes was the font, with a 'Dutch' roof over it supported by four pillars, rather like the white bell-tower above the roof. Nothing could have prepared me for the second thing, absolutely nothing; it hit me so hard that I wandered deeper in with my mouth open and my mind in a daze.

The whole church was a sea of green. Not dark green or light green: a sort of mid-range sage green. Green panelling went half way up the walls, with green broken pediments

above the entrance doors further down. The huge roof
timbers were green. The screen and the near altar rail were
green. Above the turned balustraded green screen were
three words, Holy Holy Holy, set in gold lettering into the
green. I noticed, irrelevantly, that the clerestory windows
had narrow inaccessible balconies inside and that the turned
balustrades to these were painted green. The side-aisles had
boarded barrelled ceilings on which the tongued-and-
grooved boards were white or cream but the cross-supports
at regular intervals were picked out in green. Everywhere I
looked my eye met green. Even the pews, with their turned
supports, marching down the nave in rows and set at an
angle in the aisles, were green, that mid-green, that
sage-green . . .

Suddenly, I had to sit down on one of them.

'What's the matter?' Sue's voice was curious but concerned. She spoke in a low pitch influenced by the cool green
calm of the nave and, when I didn't answer, she sat down
quickly beside me and looked into my face. 'Is it your neck?
Are you all right?'

'These pews,' I said to her in a hoarse whisper. 'They're
green. Like everything else. Look at it. Green. Sue, it's a
sort of—a sort of a *blackboard* green.'

Her eyes, peering at me, widened so that the large whites
showed in the quiet gloom.

'Are you thinking what I'm thinking?' I demanded. 'Eh?
The tin of paint at Stan Reilly's? That blackboard paint?
Middling green paint. It was just like this.'

'But, but, Tim—'

I grabbed her arm feverishly.

'We've been looking for the wrong thing! I knew it! I
knew it! You couldn't miss a thing like the V & A bookcase!
You couldn't. The police haven't found anything. Anywhere. Nor has the trade!'

'Tim—'

'Think, Sue, think! Dark green was a favourite colour of the Gothic Reformers! Morris and Company used it on their Sussex range of chairs! God damn it, Sue—'

'Tim!'

'Sorry. Sorry. But Shaw used it too! That chair! The Willesley chair in Toby's office! It's green. Rush seats and green stain: I meant to talk to Toby about corner chairs— Shaw's favourite chairs—and the ones I saw at Cragside. I forgot. Hell! I completely forgot!'

'Tim!'

'That's what Alf Brown meant. He waved offhand, Toby said, he waved or gestured at what Toby thought was the desk. The oak Gothic desk by Sedding. It wasn't that at all. He was waving at the chair, the "Queen Anne" style green chair in front of the desk! "That sort of style," he said. Toby thought he meant the desk, but the chair stands in front of it. The green chair! The—'

'Tim! Calm down! You're shaking. And repeating yourself.'

I stared at her. Then I looked around me. My neck started throbbing again and my head felt hot, even in that cool, calm, quiet green church with its three bounding Gothic arches going down each side of the aisle on their turned stone pillars.

'It was the chair. We should be looking for a darkish-green piece of furniture, Sue. Think about it: Stan Reilly's tin of paint. He must have been touching something up. He always did that in his back storeroom. We've been looking for the wrong thing. Believe me, we—'

'Tim.' Her voice was quiet but the tone made me stop, despite a desire to babble feverishly on, alone with her there in the quiet church.

'What?' I checked myself. 'What is it? Eh? Sorry—sorry. I'll speak quietly.'

'The Shaw Savill Line.' Her voice, low-toned, still conveyed a significant urgency. I scowled at her.

'What about it? What on earth has it to do with—'

'Green?'

'Sue, please!'

She grabbed my hand. 'Until it merged with the Albion Line, sometime in the early eighteen-eighties, guess what colour the ships were painted?'

I couldn't move. I couldn't believe it. 'No. It's not possible.'

'They were green. I don't know what tone but they were green. I bet it wasn't light green.'

Her hands were squeezing mine so hard my knuckles cracked and she let go. I stood up.

'Come on—quick!'

'Wait! Wait! The collection box! Please, Tim.'

I found a set of slots in the wall near the door and pressed money through the one marked 'Building Fabric'. Then I rushed through with Sue in hot pursuit.

'Where are we going? Tim!'

'To the telephone. We need Nobby. Now, quickly. Before that bloody piece of furniture vanishes forever.'

CHAPTER 17

It took ten maddening minutes to get him to the phone and then he was resentful, irascible, obstructive and downright negative. He started off badly. 'I told you,' he rasped into his end of the line, 'that I would contact you if there was any news. Toby Prescott is still semi-conscious. It isn't expected that he'll be available for at least another four hours. At least four hours. Have you got that? Four hours.'

'I don't want Toby Prescott. Or news of him. I want you.'

'Eh? What for?'

'Have you got all the files on Stan Reilly there?'

'Now look here, Tim, I've told you—'

'God damn it! Have you or haven't you? For Christ's sake, Nobby, we've been barking up the wrong tree! There is no oak Gothic piece of furniture! We should have been looking for something green!'

'What? Green? Are you drunk?'

'Dark green. Or medium green. Like the tin of blackboard paint kicked over at Stan Reilly's.'

There was a silence. Quite a long silence. Then his voice came through again, the voice of an experienced interviewer and interrogator, sober, but tinged, however, with suspicion because he was talking to me.

'What have you found out?'

'Nobby, I'm in Bedford Park. I've just been in the church. The original pews are in it, still painted green. Everything is green. All the woodwork. Everything. Norman Shaw green. The chair in Toby's office, by the desk, in the same colour. It was a favourite colour in the eighteen-sixties and 'seventies. Morris used it on rush-seated chairs. Ford Madox Ford is supposed to have made up the stain. Oh God, I'm rambling again. But that's what Alf Brown meant: he pointed at the chair and said, "That sort of style." Toby thought he meant the desk, the oak Gothic desk. It wasn't; it was the Queen Anne chair. The green one.'

There was another long silence. 'That's just guesswork,' he said eventually. 'You're guessing. Besides, I think Toby—'

'Oh God! The tin of paint at Hove was guessing, was it?' Outside the telephone-box I could see Sue, between it and the car, staring tensely at me from the pavement. The Shaw Savill colour was green; it seemed too much to be true; what a girl!

'Well, I suppose we could check.' Nobby's voice on the line was less certain, grudging.

'Now, Nobby, now! In that file you've got! Is there
anything—anything at all—that has a description
that would fit? A desk, a bookcase, a cabinet, anything?
That Stan Reilly bought in the last three months before
his death? Anything? You must have his invoices and things
there. You said he went to about six auctions. Anything
in those?'

'It'll take time. I'll have to think about it.'

'Nobby Roberts, if you don't well bloody well check *now*
I'll come round there and kill you, by God I will! There's
no time to lose! Somewhere that piece exists and is the clue
to three murderous attacks! Get off your bloody arse and
look, damn it! It won't take a minute! You've already been
through everything he bought, looking for a Gothic bookcase. Well, there isn't one; there's something else. Ninety-
nine chances out of a hundred that it's wrongly described.
You and your crowd won't know. You've *got* to tell me,
damn it! It may not give the colour! Please!'

There was a silence, another long one. Then the telephone
crackled and banged as I heard him put the receiver down
on his desk and I could hear the rustle of papers shifting.
His voice muttered resentfully in the distance. Sue still
stared at me from outside, the sun making her brown hair
shine. A great red bus thundered by, shaking the cubicle.
More paper-ruffling noises came down the line. The phone
banged again as he picked it up. His voice was almost
triumphant; he loves to prove me wrong.

'There's nothing. Nothing like that. Certainly nothing
green, anyway.'

'There has to be! What did he buy! Read all the purchase
invoices out to me!'

'Damn it, Tim, I'm supposed to be in an important
meeting!'

'Read them! There can't be that many!'

Put a man on the spot and he'll take short cuts, even if

only to save work or to get rid of someone. Nobby's voice was defensive.

'The only purchase anywhere near at all is nothing like.'

'God help me! Have you any Irish in your family? What was it?'

'A lot at Baines and Baines auction. Chipstead.'

'Chipstead? South of Croydon? Brighton direction?'

'Yes.'

'What?'

'A pair of desks. Lot 103. March sale. £375. That's all the invoice says.'

I clutched the phone. 'A pair of desks? Have you got the catalogue among his papers? He may have marked it.'

'For God's sake, Tim! What in hell?'

'Nobby! Are those two desks in his stock still? Or did he sell them? Either there's an outgoing invoice or they're still marked as in stock.'

Another silence, broken by ruffling and shifting. Another bus thundered past, followed, appropriately enough, by a Pavilion Removals van. I could have screamed.

'Odd.' Nobby's voice came back on the line. 'There's nothing in the stock. The Hove boys checked it thoroughly. But there's no sale either.'

My nerves were shaking now. I managed to get a hold of myself and sound calm. 'Nobby? See if the Baines and Baines catalogue is there? Check Lot 103. Read the description out to me.'

Another silence. Then the familiar voice. 'Well, the catalogue is here. Reilly had marked it at Lot 103 all right.'

'What does it say?'

'No luck, Tim, not on this one. Listen. Lot 103: a pair of Art Deco desks with turned supports and shelves and cupboards under and over, inscribed *ca* 1930. You see? Way out. Don't tell me that—Tim? Are you there? *Tim?*'

But I was gone by then, sprinting for the car so fast that Sue, who was nearer, only just had time to leap in and slam her door as I burnt the tyres accelerating away from the pavement.

CHAPTER 18

Chipstead is an area south of Croydon cut through by the main A23 London to Brighton road. I'd never been to it before or noticed it particularly but the location was ideal for a man like Stan Reilly who would have made regular trips through it. As we rushed towards it, weaving across from Kew Bridge and then tangling our way round Kingston and Ewell, I tried to put my thoughts in order enough to justify myself to Sue, who kept protesting about my excitement when she wasn't emitting cries of alarm at the supposed recklessness of my driving.

'Art Deco!' she kept repeating. 'What on earth are you thinking of, Tim? A pair of Art Deco desks of the nineteen-thirties! The earliest they'll be is around nineteen-twenty-five! Why the panic?'

'Look,' I said, patiently, squeezing past a bus by forcing a van up the pavement, 'you can ignore the description. They are the only things that fit. And they're missing. I must admit a pair worries me. 'Cupboards and shelves under and over.' So you know what that means? It means that they must each be a form of bureau bookcase.'

'An *Art Deco* form of bureau bookcase. Mind that old woman! Tim, that was a zebra crossing!'

'Forget the description. Out-of-town auctioneers are hopeless. Look at that duff Godwin sideboard that came up in the London Rooms a few months back. It was a copy or a fake of some sort but it was punted first in an auction in

Scotland. Do you know what it was described as in the catalogue there?'

'I remember,' she said. 'I remember well. Mind that Mini! Christ! It was listed as a wall unit.'

'There you are then. A wall unit! A Godwin sideboard, and it was a close approximation of one, catalogued as a *wall unit*. Provincial auctioneers have no expertise when.it comes to strangely-disguised furniture on the road to the Modern Movement.'

'This is hardly provincial.'

'Fringes of London. Fringes of Surrey. Call it what you like.'

'It's not Scotland. Mind that bike! The light was *red*, Tim, you were supposed to stop! The trade probably called regularly. I don't see it; I think you're grasping at straws. These people will know their stuff.'

She was wrong. Baines and Baines Auction Rooms were well off the main road through Chipstead. I had to ask twice to find them. At the end of the line of nineteen-thirties shops with metal windows there was a larger, double frontage of glass that might once have been a sizeable furnishing store. Outside, on the pavement, a wooden poster-stand proclaimed in large print that auctions were held monthly on Wednesdays and that all categories of goods, furniture, china, glass, objects of virtue, carpets and so forth were sold. Pressed to the glass frontage I could see, as I drew to a halt, the depressing accumulation of second-hand residue that comprised the Baines' catchment. There were armchairs, a sofa, ten-year-old dining chairs, a refrigerator, two oak wardrobes and a 'fifties coffee table with a broken leg. My heart sank. I got out, followed by Sue, and passed the immediate barricade of bedsitting-room rejects to enter the premises properly through the shop-door in the centre.

It was a miserable spectacle. Whatever sources Baines and Baines could tap for their sales could hardly ever have been prosperous. Boxes of cheap glassware stood on tables cluttered with dusty modern china. Spindly chairs were stacked beside electrical appliances on the dirty floor. An old porter in a long brown linen coat was pushing a broom across the far corner without enthusiasm and stared across at me without the slightest concession to hospitality.

'Too early, mate. Sale's not till next week. Viewing starts Monday. We're closed, see?'

I suppose that dealers have to cover every eventuality, every possibility, no matter how unlikely, how tedious, how demoralizing the effort can be. In all that clutter of rubbish there might be something on which a turn was possible, a Clarice Cliff pot, a Susie Cooper jug, sporting prints, a reproduction clock. Somehow this enterprise survived, vying with the local junk dealers for house clearances, probate goods, any source. Stan Reilly had come here, had bought here, not three weeks ago.

'Is the manager in?' Behind the far wall was an office-window through which I could see shelves of box-files, an electric fan.

'Nah. He's out.' The sweeping stopped and the old porter looked at me steadily without sympathy. Sue picked up a glass vase and a look of irritation crossed his face. 'Not on view yet, miss. Monday. Next Monday.'

There was only one way to deal with him. I got out my wallet and walked across to him, taking a blue five-pound note out of it clearly in full view, so that his eyes narrowed and then softened as he watched me.

'I'm looking into something on Stan Reilly's behalf. You knew Stan? From Hove.'

If Stan Reilly had bought here he must have dropped in regularly. The chances were he'd tipped this porter from time to time, asked him to leave bids. The face was lined and stubbly, pale with lack of exposure to the light, but the old man's body was lean and stringy, a body used to lifting with economy of effort, efficient leverage, careful movement. I guessed that he'd been a porter for many years.

'Stan Reilly? Yes, 'course I knew Stan. You're not police.' The statement came factually, watching the blue banknote. His eyes flicked to Sue, to make sure she wasn't pinching the lots.

'No. I'm an old friend. In the trade. London.'

He nodded, leaning on broom. 'Someone done him in. Last week.'

'I know. He bought two desks here last month. Your last sale.'

The old head nodded again.

'The catalogue says they were Art Deco. What were they like?'

A broad grin parted the grey-stubbled face, revealing yellow teeth that were surprisingly even but not false. He jerked a thumb at the vacant manager's office behind him and a look of scorn replaced the grin.

'He's a bloody fool, he is. Got no idea. Never been in the trade. Thinks anyone can set up and run an auction. Bloody fool.'

'Were they not Art Deco?'

'Haven't you seen them?' The eyes went sharp, resting full on my face.

'No. They've gone missing. That's why I'm here.' I put my wallet away and passed him the note. 'I just need a proper description. That's why I'm here.'

He took the note and palmed it down into his coat pocket with a single movement. His head jerked back towards the office of the absent manager. 'I *told* him they wasn't Art Deco. Bloody fool. He wouldn't know. I was thirty years in this trade, porter in the West End rooms, see? I knows antique furniture when I sees it. Retired here, I did. Took this job to help out, keep me in beer money. Fool. Just 'cos they was a bit different, bit odd, he calls them Art Deco.

Art Deco my arse, I says, but it was too late then. He'd sent the catalogue off to print. Too proud, anyway. Wouldn't change because of me.'

'What were they?'

He grinned. 'Stan Reilly knew. Knew as soon as he saw them. Art Deco he says to me, Christ, some Art Deco. I know, I says, they were never twentieth-century, those. That's that Art furniture, I says, ain't it, and he grins and says keep it to yourself as usual, and I did. He was good that way, Stan, there was always a bit in it for you if you looked after him, see?'

'Art furniture? You mean like that late nineteenth-century Victorian stuff?'

'Yeah. What do they call it now. Ess something. Ess-thetic, is it?'

I felt a dreadful block of disappointment raise itself in me. 'Not Aesthetic Movement?'

'Yeah. That's it. Aesthetic Movement. You know, they 'ad shelves and doors and panels and things. They had a funny top, tall they were, with a sort of balcony. Fussy, I call them. Never liked that stuff meself.'

I sighed, feeling my shoulder slump. Another dead end. 'Aesthetic Movement. You mean they were ebonized? Black lacquered?'

His jaw muscles clamped angrily. 'I know what ebonized means! 'Course they wasn't ebonized! Black? Who buys black? Eh? Trade don't like black, do they? Stan Reilly wouldn't have bought black, now would he? What would he do with that black stuff?'

'I—I'm sorry. Didn't mean to upset you. It's just that m st of the Aesthetic Movement furniture is black, so naturally I —what were they then? Oak?'

'Nah! Oak! 'Course not! Would *he* have catalogued them as Art Deco if they'd been oak? It was the colour that fooled him, see? Green, they were. Darkish green, well, a sort of

mid-green I suppose, like that bloody awful carpet over
there. Funny furniture, I says, painted green like that, but
Stan liked them and he got them even though the two local
boys bid him up to nearly four hundred. Art Deco! *He* thinks
that anything green like that has got to be nineteen-thirties,
he does.'

Sue's face was a picture. Come to think of it, mine must
have been quite a sight. I could practically hear my heart
thumping. 'Green? Good God. Where did they come from?'

The answer was prompt. 'Depository. Croydon way. We
got a load of old stuff they'd had since the war. No claimants.
Turned it out to get rid of it. Some good armchairs there
were, and some office furniture, way out of date. Wooden
filing cabinets. Didn't fetch much. Only the desks.'

'Green.' Sue's voice was full of wonder. 'Green bureau
bookcases.'

The old head shook vigorously. 'Nah. Not bureaus. No
bureau, see? Desk, it was. Desktop, sticking out. Didn't have
a fall, like a bureau. Didn't have to open it, see, miss, it was
fixed. Made special for someone, I reckon. Heavy, they
were. Gone missing, have they? Rare lot to go missing, I
reckon. How'd they do that? Lose 'em? Someone scarper
with the whole load, I suppose? Happens quite a bit nowadays. Or did they just ship 'em by mistake?'

My mouth was dry. 'No,' I said. 'I don't think they were
lost or shipped. At least I hope not. Not yet.'

He shook his head. 'Bloody amazing. It'd have to be a
big bush to lose those under. Mind you,' he chuckled, 'they
did have their initials on 'em. Maybe someone'd lost them
before.'

'Initials? What initials?'

'Up top. Inscribed, wasn't they. With initials.'

'They weren't—they weren't R.N.S., were they? The
initials, I mean?'

'Nah.' He shook his head again. 'Nothing like that. There

was a 'W' in them. Don't remember the others; I didn't
really bother. Don't like that stuff. But they were different.
Not the same.' His face took on a disgruntled look. 'Don't
get much worth anything here. Load of bloody rubbish.
Look at it.'

'Er—yes. Thanks. Thanks a lot. We must go.'

I took Sue's arm carefully and steered her to the door.
'Thanks,' I called back to the old porter again, but he'd
already started his sweeping and made no response as he
created more dust particles to settle on the glass, the china
and the used, unlovely furnishings stacked in that unlikely
birthplace of a violent resurrection. A thought struck me
and I put my head back through the door.

'Was it you who helped Stan on with them?'

The brushing stopped. He stared at me with almost the
contempt he'd had for his manager. 'On with them? What
d'you mean, on with them?'

'Load them up. On to his estate car.'

The yellow, even teeth appeared again in a broad grin.
'Them two bits wouldn't even go on Stan's brake. Never.
You should've seen 'em, mate. Nah. He got a carrier to pick
'em up next day.'

'A carrier? Stan usually took things himself, on his Granada.'

'Well, he didn't take these, I'm telling you, mate, 'cos I
helped with 'em on myself.'

'On what? Whose?'

'Eh?'

'You helped who? Who were the carriers?'

'The London-Brighton boys. The regular run. He used
'em before. Trade all use them. They didn't lose them, did
they? Big pieces like those?'

'Who? For Christ's sake, who?'

He glared at me angrily and gripped his brush in self-
defence.

'The one they all use, of course! Who the bloody hell else? The trade boys: Pavilion Removals, mate.'

CHAPTER 19

'Instead of one combined operation,' I spoke out loud, 'we have two separate ones. Life's often like that, you said.'

She didn't answer. I had made the mistake of sitting in the Jaguar at the kerb for a few minutes to try and get my thoughts straight. Sue had gone completely silent and waited for me without expression, staring ahead into a far distance that obviously didn't contain our surroundings in Chipstead within it. Occasionally her brow furrowed. I got out my briefcase, opened a file, read carefully, closed it and looked across at her as I replaced the briefcase.

'We're parked on a double yellow line,' she said. 'And I'm completely lost. I don't know how those two desk-bookcases fit but I take back what I said. It's incredible. Green. All the time: all the time we were looking, we'd missed the obvious thing from the start.'

'Stan's tin of paint.'

'Yes.' She put her hand on mine. 'What are you going to do now?'

'I think I know where those things are. Might be. Possibly.'

'Where?'

I started the engine. 'I think we'll go and look. Right now.'

Wrong now. I said that I made the mistake of sitting at the kerb to think and a mistake it was. A minute earlier and I'd have been clear, but the dark Rover cut across my path so quickly and stopped so close that it was almost touching. Sue let out a strangled cry of shock but I was out of the car by then and my feet must have hit the ground at the same moment as the two men who sprang from the Rover. I found myself, fists bunched, face to face with Nobby Roberts. Behind him stood a dark-suited bloke with a hard-packed physique that I didn't like the look of at all. Not at all. I let my fists slacken.

'Caught you,' said Nobby, his face right in mine. 'Almost got away, didn't you? Mind you, I'd have been here five minutes ago if there hadn't been a march through Parliament Square.'

'Good driver, is he?'

'One of the best. Grabbed him as soon as you rang off on me. You bugger.' His voice carried no resentment: it was just flat and uncommitted, official. 'I ought to arrest you.'

'What for?'

'Obstruction. Or something like it.'

'Solving your cases for you, you mean? Saving you from making a fool of yourself?'

He grinned. 'Jumping the gun again, Tim? The case isn't solved yet. And I'm not pleased. I'm not pleased because you've tried to rush off on your own to muddy the waters and I'm not pleased because you've got Sue with you and we are dealing with a very dangerous criminal. So tell me all.'

'Otherwise?'

'Otherwise I shall tell my driver here, who happens to be a very good detective-constable, to arrest you and lock you away in the nearest nick. I mean it. Then I shall go into those auction rooms—if they can really be called that—and find out what you've found out and why it's made you keen to go careering off again so urgently and where to.'

'You won't, because you won't be able to put two and two together the way I can from my angle.'

'But I'll have you in chokey and I'll demand that you tell me.'

There's nothing you can do with Nobby when he's in one of his high-handed, official moods so I sighed, nodded acceptance, and made him a proposal. 'Why don't you follow me and I'll explain when we get to the bookcases, or where I think they are?'

He shook his head. 'I don't trust you. It isn't that you are good enough to shake off my driver but you might play a trick of some sort. So I'll offer you a deal: you and Sue get in the back of *my* car and you can be telling me all about it while we drive to wherever you tell my driver to go.'

I sighed. 'OK. But I'll have to move my car. It's on a double yellow line.'

He held out his hand. 'Just give me the keys. My driver will park it for you while you get in the Rover. Both of you.' He held Sue's door open and ignored her expression. 'Hello, Sue. This way, please. If you don't mind.'

So that was it. We piled into Nobby's police car, a police car without signs or flashing lights, and his driver parked mine and came back with a satisfied look on his face as he returned the keys. Then I gave him instructions and, as we drove back to the A23 and the motorway, I told Nobby what we had found out, where we had got to and why I thought what I did. He sat listening attentively and asked very few questions; even the driver asked one or two and they were pretty intelligent so I hoped that I'd given them a reasonable view by the time we turned in past the gates by the picturesque lodge with its white-painted windows.

'Not the house,' I said to the back of the driver's head as the tower came into sight. 'Keep on round the house till you come to the stable block. That's where we stop.'

We pulled up in the weed-scattered yard and clambered out in front of the big diagonal-planked doors under the clock. There were lights on in the office-block but no windows from that side gave on to the stableyard and it was curiously quiet and shadowed, out of the sun; a cold yard, I thought.

'They don't look as though they've been opened for years,' said Nobby, prowling along the line of high doors. 'No: wait a moment. These have been moved.'

There was a padlock and hasp securing the double set from the outside and Nobby hesitated for a moment. He gave me a very keen stare. 'You reckon this is it?'

I hesitated for just a moment. 'I—I think so.'

He nodded at his driver, who walked across, looked at the padlock, smiled a faint smile, took out a bunch of spidery keys, fiddled about for a minute and then clicked the padlock open. We all grasped the doors and swung them wide apart.

'A pantechnicon,' said Sue, her voice surprised. 'What on earth is it doing here? It's enormous.'

'Pavilion Removals.' Nobby's voice was soft as he looked at me. 'That fits.'

The back of the huge van was locked too, with a padlock, but the policeman made even less work of that. We let down the back flap and pushed the big roller blind up out of the way so that we could clamber in unobstructed. It was quite light enough to see what we wanted to see but Nobby's man, efficient as ever, went back to the car and fetched a torch.

They were about eight feet high; high enough to look impressive but not too high for most ceilings; certainly not for Victorian ones. They stood facing each other across the van floor, strapped by canvas webbing to the side battens so that they wouldn't fall over. As your eye went naturally from the projecting writing surface that each had—for they were identical—it followed the lines of the vertical divisions set in the left-hand side of the upper half, rested on the green fielded door to the right, rose to an arched gallery under the top balustrade and then saw the dark, tiled roof set back from the balustrade, like a seventeenth-century house which has had a Georgian façade added to it. Then your eye went back to the writing surface, which was fixed and permanent, supported by green, turned pillars, and you remembered that the fall-front bureau was right out of fashion in the eighteen-sixties and eighteen-seventies, so that even though the designer was emulating the great bureau-bookcases of the 'Queen Anne' period he still could not bring himself to include a fall front and had instead made this a gentle, fixed slope with tooled leather set in the green surround.

Each piece was about three feet six inches wide and, beneath the writing surface, set back under the slope, were more shelves and cupboards with arched, fielded panels to the doors that emulated the curves above. The green stain was scuffed here and there but it was the same tone as the pews in St Michael's church and I had the impression of looking at a similar combination of Gothic sentiment, conveyed by the slatted-tile roof, stained nearly black, and 'Queen Anne' styling that I had noticed in Bedford Park. Incised lines in various surfaces showed remnants of subtle gilding deep in their recesses where some part of the design, some emphasis of decoration, had been carefully strengthened to the eye. But it was above the upper gallery of four arches, just below the roof balustrade, that my gaze went to the faded gold initials: J.W.T. on one and there, opposite, W.S. on the other. Sue did one of her sketches later and it was the initials that she, too, remembered so vividly; the Leyswood ones, as it happened.

I found that the other three were staring at me, waiting expectantly for an explanation, so I pointed at the initials in turn.

'James William Temple,' I said, my voice sounding unexpectedly loud inside the van, 'and Walter Savill. J.W.T. and W.S. The partners in the Shaw Savill line when Norman Shaw built the new "Queen Anne" offices in Leadenhall Street. And designed these bureau-bookcases, partners' desks, whatever you want to call them, for their big semi-circular office on the first floor back. One each, with their initials. I bet his own stamp is somewhere on them.'

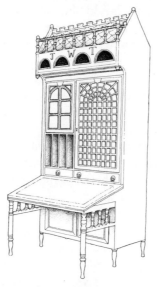

I looked closely at the writing-slope on the nearest desk, tracing the green-painted wooden surround with my fingers. At the top, in the centre, just where each partner would have looked every time he used the surface, I saw the faint impression stamped into the green surface: R.N.S. It was the same stamp that had been so prominently placed on Toby's chair, between my legs, with its five 'rays' fanned out in a tiny sunburst above the initials set in an arched rectangle. I stared up at the balustrade around the sloping 'roof' which replaced the double domes or the parapeted mouldings of real Queen Anne furniture. A 'roof' on a piece like this had more to it than an architectural effect, more than a genuflection in the direction of Gothic. It had a vaguely sinister, very grave, almost threatening air about it that reminded me of the ominous roofs over the tower at Leyswood. It hinted at protection, fortification, in an armed

way that conveyed grim strength to the approaching way-
farer. Had they been sitting at these desks, bookcases,
whatever description should fit, when the news came
through? Sailing ships were not for men with weak stomachs.
Somehow the work of Shaw, the artistic interest of the chase,
had made me forget the real courage that created the wealth
for those great houses, those happy artistic indulgences. The
Cospatrick had foundered only a year after they had moved
into Shaw's light-hearted building in Leadenhall Street;
they bought the old frigate-built ship at the time of their
move. Had the partners come back then, after the dreadful
details had emerged, to sit at these desks in horrified silence,
with the rhythm of Gilbert's gruesome, mock-macabre
humour beating in their minds?

> *The next lot fell to the Nancy's mate*
> *And a delicate dish he made:*
> *Then our appetite with the midshipmite*
> *We seven survivors stayed.*

Nineteenth century shipowners needed strong consti-
tutions and hard fists; there is a thesis to be written sometime, not by me, on the relationship between art and
commerce, a relationship which Temple and Savill were
unlikely to dwell upon. They would not have had much time
for the Arthurian fantasies of the well-heeled Morris and his
circle; it was no wonder that the practical but cheerful Shaw,
with his easy understanding of armaments manufacturers
and other big shipowners, was their man. At these pieces of
furniture they had probably run their company for many
years after the building of New Zealand Chambers, facing
other disasters, human and financial, until the 'nineties, by
which time both men were gone. I wondered how much
they had used the desks, whether they had liked them,
whether the cousin and the dead brother's partner had

appreciated them and found them practical. Shaw himself, fit, devout, sensible, had lived on until 1912, so he would have known if the desks had been relinquished. By then perhaps he would not have cared, for he had become a Classical reviver and said that the Gothic was dead. I did know, whatever their history, that I was looking at two very important pieces of furniture, things worth murder to a dedicated man, or a greedy one, and that poor Alf Brown and Stan Reilly might have guessed what they had found.

'What the hell is going on? What are you doing here?' The voice, angry and hoarse, broke my reverie and the silent examination the others were making. Peter Coe, tall and angular, stood in the double doorway holding a shotgun whose bright double-barrels pointed at me as the nearest person. There were no country tweeds on him this time, no mud-stained clothes: he was in a working suit. 'Who gave you permission to break in here?'

There was a moment's silence as I sensed Sue moving guiltily behind me. Nobby and his man didn't move.

'Pigeon-shooting?' I don't know why I get flippant on these occasions, I think it's probably nerves; I just can't help it. It could have been elation, though: elation at seeing a great dark bruise on his cheek.

'You.' The word contained great hatred. 'Simpson. You haven't bought us yet, you know!' The voice rose to a shout. 'You're trespassing! I could—I—' The gun moved as his arm tensed and I heard Nobby step quietly out beside me.

'Mr Peter Coe?'

He got a livid glare. 'Who the hell are you? Another of White's vultures?'

'I am a police officer. I am making inquiries into the deaths of Alfred Brown in Long Acre, London, and Stan Reilly, antique dealer of Hove, within the last three weeks.'

The voice had become official, flat, a monotone carefully devoid of emphasis or emotion. Coe stared at him in disbelief for a moment, flicked his eyes sideways to the plain-coloured unbadged Rover and then back to me, Sue, the other two men. He jerked the shotgun in a spasmodic movement.

'Rubbish! I know what you are! Traders! Working with White's Art Fund. You're trespassers!' He glared at me again, swinging the double-barrels back with the line of his eyes.

'Were you on the van when it picked them up? At Baines and Baines?'

He didn't answer or blink.

'Doing one of your checks? On distribution patterns and timing?'

No sound.

'I think you must have been. You knew immediately what these were, or you guessed pretty closely.'

His eyes narrowed at me. For a moment I thought he was going to fire. 'I haven't the faintest idea what you mean.'

'The Orchard is in Bedford Park,' I said, not flippantly.

The eyes widened, losing focus. 'Eh? What?'

'You said you lived in Acton Green. I wondered why you didn't want me to look up your address. Technically, you are on the edge of Acton Green. But when I looked it up, The Orchard struck a bell. It's on the western side of Bedford Park. The place you don't want to leave, despite your wife. Beautiful houses, aren't they?'

He licked his lips. I could practically hear the numbed mind's mechanism whirring for answers.

'I suppose you've always been keen on Norman Shaw? Living in Bedford Park? When you saw them being carried into the van you must have had a very good idea what they were? Green, like the woodwork in St Michael's? Wouldn't Stan Reilly sell them to you? Or did he sell them but want too much? He must have helped you, the second time. The time you took them out of his store and put them in this van. Pavilion called on Stan regularly; no one remarked on that particular visit. Rather like the milkman in a Father Brown story. You murdered Stan Reilly for them. And you tried to murder me; you thought I was much nearer to them than I really was. I suppose Alf Brown was an accident? Wouldn't he go back on his agreement with Stan?'

He cleared his throat. 'I don't know what you're talking about.'

'Then how did these get here? Only twenty miles from Hove? To a building you knew had been unused for years and wasn't likely to be? And how did you get that bruise on your cheek?'

He licked his lips. 'This is fantastic. You've no evidence.'

'Tons of it. The forensic evidence, that is. Your hair on Toby Prescott's door-jamb, for instance.'

There was silence. Uncertainty etched into his face. Nobby suddenly couldn't stand it any more. He stepped forward and Coe waved the shotgun.

'Don't move!'

'Peter Coe, I must ask you to accompany me to answer inquiries connected with the murder of Stan Reilly at Hove. I must warn you that you are not obliged to say anything but that anything you do say may be taken down in evidence.'

'Stay where you are!'

Nobby paid no attention. 'Put that down,' he snapped. 'If you put that down now, I shall simply accept that we met while you were intending to go pigeon-shooting and say no more.'

'No!'

'There are four of us here. And God knows how many people in the offices behind you.'

'Stay where you are! God! Simpson!' Suddenly the shot-gun swung back to me. 'I'm warning you, I—I'll kill you!' Tears began to run from his eyes. 'I'll kill you! I will!'

I shook my head. I don't know why, but I'd never felt more exuberant. 'Not a hope. You'd have done it by now, if you could. You only get one chance at a pigeon. You should know that.'

'Put it down! I am warning you!' Nobby's voice rasped nervously. 'We are police officers! We are armed! Put it down!'

Armed. Turning fractionally to my left I knew, now, why I hadn't felt comfortable about the look of Nobby's driver. Trust Nobby: he'd brought his hard man with him and his hard man was standing at the edge of the van, apart, with a clear vision to Coe. A black police revolver was in his hand now; no expression altered his unemotional face. He stared straight at Peter Coe without moving or even bothering to bring his handgun up into both hands in the normal firing position. The double-barrels moved, swung, wavered and then dipped, despondently. The head behind them drooped. Nobby tramped down the sloping back-flap to the ground and took the shotgun from Coe without resistance.

'Very sensible,' he said, taking an arm and turning back to beckon the silent driver. 'You wouldn't have got half way to squeezing the trigger before he shot you, Mr Coe. Assuming that this is loaded. Is it?'

CHAPTER 20

Jeremy White's drawing-room on the first floor of his house in Kensington is an elegant room overlooking the square-cum-crescent filled with trees outside. There were four couples there that evening: Jeremy and Mary, of course; myself and Sue; Nobby and Gillian, lending, as Jeremy facetiously put it, an air of respectability to what would otherwise have been a raffish gathering, and Toby Prescott, together with a very voluptuous Resting Actress who had put her hand on my arm three times that evening in dramatically affectionate gestures which caused Sue to produce glacial glares and to stiffen as though someone had stuck an easel down her back. Not that there was anything for her to worry about; the Resting Actress was, quite clearly, totally taken with Toby and was merely showing me friendship in that tangibly insincere way that theatre people have. Toby and I were examining Jeremy's paintings together while the rest of the group lingered over port or 'stickies', as Jeremy described his liqueurs.

'Thomas Whitcombe,' murmured Toby, hospital plaster still adorning his forehead. 'A frigate off the Cape. Very nice. Very expensive.'

'Quite appropriate, too, if about a hundred years premature. The *Cospatrick* was a frigate-built ship.'

'Really, Tim. If every time one looks at a fine eighteenth-century marine painting of a frigate one is going to be reminded of that ghastly disaster, life will be impossible.'

'Sorry. It just happened to be off the Cape and a frigate. That's what reminded me. Nothing else. Whitcombe is a fine painter.'

'Indeed. And so formal. Think what a dramatic fiasco an artist of the eighteen-seventies would have made of the subject.'

I laughed. 'You mean Clarkson Stanfield or Cooke or one of those?'

'Well—I wasn't going to—knowing your—'

I laughed again. 'You won't upset me by saying that eighteenth-century marine painting is superior to nineteenth. I might agree with you.'

'What an easy fellow you are to get on with. Not like the old Tim at all.'

'Thanks.'

He giggled. 'I suppose you won't lend me any money now?'

'Not a penny. But I fancy Jeremy will.'

'Dear Jeremy. He's obviously as pleased as punch about buying this timber firm of Coe's. And about the bookcases. I've never seen him look so successful.'

'Indeed. Now is the time to touch him for a loan for your bookshop if ever there was one. I'm very sorry about Alf Brown, Toby; it seems that Peter Coe, having seen Stan Reilly about the bookcases and been told that Alf was trawling for a buyer, tried to dissuade Alf from bringing you and me in to counter-bid. Alf knew, though, that he was likely to get a much better offer if we were given a chance. They had a row and Coe lost his temper. Nobby tells me that he would have got off with a manslaughter plea for that one; he didn't mean to kill Brown. But then he was in a fix; he went back to see Stan, persuaded him to let him buy the pieces and they loaded them up in the Pavilion Removals van that Coe had brought. Coe was in overalls, like an employee; he knew that Stan would soon put two and two together so he strangled Stan and drove off in the van like any delivery man, and put it in the stables. He was the distribution director, after all; when anyone queried where the vehicle was he told them he had it out on special loan. Nothing unusual about that in transport firms. All he needed to do when things died down was get a man from his firm, drive to wherever he intended to keep the pieces and get the man to help unload. Bob's your uncle. No one was looking for two green desk-cabinets, were they?'

Toby shook his head. 'It's quite horrifying. It could easily have worked.'

'It certainly could. We were all barking up a Gothic gum-tree.'

'Ah no!' He patted my arm. 'You would have got to it, Tim, in the end. No one escapes the Simpson curiosity.' He giggled again.

'Toby! Cut it out! Actually, it was extraordinary. Those pieces must have been taken out of Leadenhall Street at the beginning of the war and put in a depository for safe keeping. Bang down come the incendiary bombs in 1941 and records get lost. Hence the disappearance. Hence the eventual clearance and sale as Art Deco desks. Amazing.'

'And the Art Fund is certain of title?'

'Oh yes. The lawyers are quite clear. Stan Reilly bought them fair and square at auction and the depository owners, who are now as sick as parrots, were perfectly entitled to dispose of them after storage for so long. We have them from Stan's estate and, I may say, you will get your introductory fee. Some small compensation for the bang on the head.'

He touched the plaster automatically. 'I suppose I was lucky. It was you Coe was after. He must hate you on two counts: the family business and the cabinets. You were influential in depriving him of both as he seems to see it.'

I looked down at the carpet. 'He's wrong about the business, of course. That was between Sir John and Jeremy. I was just the runner in that one. But he obviously saw me as a threat to the Shaw cabinets and the timber thing simply added to my undesirability overall. He must have followed me to your offices that evening in absolutely reckless despair. When I went to the loo, he pounced.'

'Indeed. Just after you'd gone in I remembered there was no soap. I went out to the reception area to get a bar and there was this tall man I'd never seen before. I still don't remember anything after that.'

'He hit you with all the force of a seething maniac and then tried to strangle me. We're both lucky, Toby, not just you.'

'Tim! Toby!' Jeremy's voice sang across the room. 'Stop murmuring together.' He put down his glass and came across to us. 'And stop looking at my Whitcombe so covetously. You look as though you're plotting something.'

'Oh no.' I grinned at him. 'We were just discussing Toby's plans to expand the business.'

'Ah! Ah!' Jeremy was suddenly all attention. He beamed in a proprietorial fashion at Toby and put an arm around his shoulders. 'Of course, Toby, my dear fellow, of course. We must get together at the Bank and discuss it. We will be glad—of course we will, won't we, Tim?—to help you finance your expansion. Just the thing for White's. Publishing and book-dealing: I have some rather special ideas I'd like to put to you. Profitable ideas. One or two contacts of mine that might help *The Modern Façade* considerably. Eh, Tim?'

'Oh, er, yes,' I responded obediently, noting a slight expression of alarm cross Toby's face and then quickly disappear as he nodded at Jeremy.

'Super. Great. I'd love that. There's only likely to be one condition I'll insist upon if White's come in with finance—at the right price, of course.'

Jeremy stared at him. 'What's that?'

'That I can have Tim on the board as a non-executive director. I think I can trust him to look after things.'

I was so taken aback that my jaw must have dropped. Jeremy burst out into one of his high-pitched arpeggios of laughter as he wagged a finger at us. 'I knew it! I knew you were plotting! But of course! How very appropriate! I entirely agree; we would like someone to look after our interests if we finance a major expansion and I know Tim needs a change from timber. He finds it boring, you know, Toby, unless it's built into bookcases.' He leant forward confidentially. 'As a matter of fact so do I, but don't tell anyone at White's. They think I'm dreadful enough already.' He gave us an unrepentant grin. 'But enough of business; it's time we looked after the ladies.'

And so that was it, until the party broke up and we all made our different ways home. I let Sue into the flat and we sat and sipped coffee under the big marine painting that had acquired, like all nineteenth-century marine paintings, a different significance for me now. She gave me one of her looks.

'You are a dreadfully acquisitive bunch,' she said. 'You've acquired a timber business, a removal business, a Gothic house in Sussex, two desk-cabinets by Norman Shaw and now probably a stake in a magazine and an antiquarian bookshop. What will you want to possess next?'

I put down my coffee. 'I can't answer for White's,' I said, moving across to her. 'But for myself I have absolutely no doubt whatsoever.'

ABOUT THE AUTHOR

JOHN MALCOLM is a founding member of the Antique Collector's Club and has authored several price guides to antique furniture. A graduate of Cambridge University, he lives in England. He is the author of *Whistler in the Dark, The Gwen John Sculpture, The Godwin Sideboard,* and *A Back Room in Somers Town.*